Love Revival

Can this widow find love again?

A complete Christian romance for adults. Warning: contains love making scenes before marriage with a couple who end up getting married.

Jade's faith has been tested.

A widow from a mentally and physically abusive husband, she now has the chance to start over again.

Moving in with her aunt seemed like the best way to get away from men and find her path again, but getting a job as the Pastor's secretary could be what starts a love like no other.

John the Pastor soon falls in love with Jade's abruptness and no rubbish attitude, and Jade starts to warm to him too.

But after being burnt so badly in her last marriage, will she be willing to allow love to revive in her again?

Find out in this new heartfelt romance by Shannon Gardener of BWWM Club.

Suitable for over 18s only due to sex scenes between a Christian couple.

Tip: Search **BWWM Club** on Amazon to see more of our great books.

Get Free Romance eBooks!

Hi there. As a special thank you for buying this book, for a limited time I want to send you some great ebooks completely **free of charge** directly to your email! You can get it by going to this page:

www.saucyromancebooks.com/physical

You can see a the cover of these books on the next page:

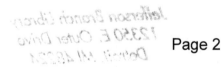

Page 2

These ebooks are so exclusive you can't even buy them. When you download them I'll also send you updates when new books like this are available.

Again, that link is:

www.saucyromancebooks.com/physical

ISBN-13: 978-1517542566

ISBN-10: 1517542561

Contents

Chapter 1

"My dear, what on earth are you doing to the poor soil?"
Selene Wright closed the gate hurriedly and came over to the
girl sitting on the ground; digging furiously with a small trowel.

"Getting the soil ready for spring, Aunt Selene," Jade looked
up with a slight smile. At least she'd had the good sense to
cover her hair with a large straw hat. She had gardening
gloves on and her clothes were old and dirt streaked.

"So you're a gardener now?" Selene asked her in amusement.

Jade shrugged and poured some seedlings into the hole she
had dug and covered the hole with the dirt heaped at the side.
"I was getting a little bored, so I figured I would occupy
myself."

"Come inside dear, we need to talk and my throat feels a little
parched from talking all day," Selene walked towards the
house. The day was lovely and it was getting a little cold as it
was nearly five o'clock.

Jade dragged off her work gloves and placed them along with
the trowel on the column of the porch. She had prepared a

simple meal of canned soup and some of the bread her aunt had baked yesterday. Mondays were left over day and she had found some lasagna in the fridge as well. She wasn't a great cook and she hated the kitchen but she figured it was the least she could do.

She came downstairs, freshly showered and in an old T-shirt to find her aunt in the kitchen making a salad. "You look so much better with all that dirt gone from your skin," she indicated for her niece to take a seat at the small kitchen table.

Selene shared a plate and put it in front of her niece. "Eat," she ordered.

"I have a solution to your problem," Selene began as she shared a plate and came to join her.

"Which one?" Jade raised a finely arched brow.

Selene laughed and gave her a searching glance. As always, it amazed her how beautiful yet how sad the girl looked. She had come to live with her for the last two weeks and she found herself wondering what to do about her situation. "Your unemployment problem," Selene dug her fork into her salad.

She had poured two small bowls of the soup and placed them on the table as well.

"You have a job for me?" Jade's large dark eyes looked a little interested.

"Yes, you are a qualified secretary and my church office needs one. Dear Sister Francis has retired and has gone away to care for her sick sister; so there's an opening."

"A church office?" Jade put down her fork, her brow furrowed. She had not been to church in a long time and even though her aunt had tried to get her to go, she had made up some sort of excuse; she was just not ready to face people yet; especially people in a small town who look at you curiously as if they wanted you to spill your guts to them.

"The young minister, a delightful young man who took over from his father when Pastor John died last year needs help in the office and the poor thing is just finding his way around the church and its environs." Selene continued, ignoring the frown on her niece's face. The girl had suffered so many tragedies in her young life; first her mother, Selene's sister dying of cancer three years ago and then barely celebrating her one year anniversary two years ago and her young husband dying in a car crash. No wonder she never smiled. But God did not give a person more than they could bear, she thought with a sigh. "You start tomorrow."

"Do I have a say in this?" Jade looked at her aunt with a bland stare.

"None whatsoever dear," Selene reached out and closed a hand over the Jade's that was resting on the table. "It's time to start living again." She added softly.

*****

That night in her room, she sat at the dressing table staring into the mirror. She reached up her hands to lift her heavy shoulder length curls and put it on top of her head; she had been meaning to cut it but had not got around to doing it and now it was getting unruly. Her caramel colored skin showed no signs of the extreme stress she had been through over the years. Her husband had always sat her down on the bed and stared at her like a piece of meat. Michael Reid – people think that she was mourning the loss of her husband but she had never revealed the ugly truth to anyone; she had felt a tremendous sense of relief when he had died. He had turned into the worse kind of minister as soon as the ink had dried on their marriage certificate and had abused her physically and mentally for the entire time they had been married. She was not mourning the loss of her husband; she was feeling guilty because she felt like throwing a party to celebrate that he was gone.

*****

Jade looked at herself critically for a moment. She had spent half an hour trying to figure out what one wears to a church office and then she figured that an office was an office and the usual get up was quite appropriate. She smoothed her hands over her pin striped black and white skirt suit; wondering if her pencil slim skirt was too short. She had wound her hair in a thick bun on top of her head in frustration and applied a minimum amount of make-up.

"You look gorgeous!" Selene exclaimed as she came into the kitchen. She was already dressed for work; in a purple skirt and white top with a light purple sweater over it. Her aunt was a second grade teacher at the local school and she was totally dedicated to her job. Jade had often wondered if that was the reason she had never gotten married or had children.

"Thanks aunty," Jade accepted the cup of coffee gratefully; eyeing the stack of pancakes speculatively. Her stomach was jumping too much to accept any food.

"Aren't you going to eat something?" Aunt Selene asked, coming to the table with two glasses of orange juice in her hands.

"I am way too nervous to eat," Jade admitted ruefully. She had taken a seat and cupped the mug in her hands.

"You have nothing to be nervous about dear," Selene gave an encouraging smile, pushing the plate towards her.

With a reluctant laugh, Jade dug into the pancakes. "I can never get mine to come out so fluffy," She murmured actually enjoying the pancakes.

"It has to do with the amount of milk and eggs you put in," Selene watched as she swirled the pancakes around the maple syrup. The girl was way too thin, she thought as if life had beaten her down somewhat. It was her intention to put some flesh on her bones. She was so hauntingly beautiful with such an ethereal delicacy.

"I am not much of a cook," Jade admitted with a shrug.

"I am a great cook, so we make a good team," Selene told her cheerfully; causing Jade to laugh.

Jade drove behind her aunt to the church office. The church building was small and quaint and the yard boasts a church hall; a three bedroom cottage for the Minister and an office attached. The parking lot had several cars parked there and her aunt told her that on Tuesday mornings they had prayer meetings.

The office was surprisingly large and well furnished.

"You thought it would be impoverished," Aunt Selene said in amusement, seeing the expression on her face. "It has several outreach programs like a day care kindergarten and a soup kitchen where the homeless are fed every day; it's quite a busy place my dear." She went ahead and knocked on the big oak door facing the inner office.

"Come in," a male voice called out.

A young man came from around the massive desk and Jade's eyes widened as she realized the color of his skin was white.

"Sister Selene, good to see you," he came around and took her aunt's hands in his.

"Pastor John, this is my niece Jade Reid I spoke to you about," Selene told him. He turned towards her and Jade found herself looking into a pair of dark green eyes; the shade of a forest on a rainy day. His hair was more blonde than brown and he had a healthy shade of tan that he surely had not gotten it from sitting in a church office or whatever it was that pastors did.

"Why don't you take a seat and we will talk," he indicated the chairs in front of the desk. Selene declined saying that she was running a little late for work. "I'll see you later dear," she told Jade, heading for the door.

Jade handed him her folder with her documents.

"I see you are a qualified secretary," he commented leafing through her documents. "We will not be able to pay you what you are worth Ms. Reid but we run a professional organization here and we expect that the work will get done."
"I am nothing if not professional," Jade told him coolly. "And I am here because I need something to do for now."

"It seems to me that you don't want to be here, do you?" he asked her bluntly.

"That's beside the point right now, Mr.?" she paused and looked at him. "I don't think calling you 'Pastor John' is quite appropriate seeing as I am not one of your flocks."

"My name is John Wynter, Ms. Reid," he told her stiffly. "And I am asking again, do you want to be here?"

"I am here and I am very good at what I do so that should be enough for now." She responded.

He stared at her for a moment then he stood, He looked way too hot to be a pastor, she thought with an inward grimace. She stood with him and preceded him to the outer office. "Sister Bailey left everything in order and the filing is up to date." He indicated the desk where Jade was surprised to see the latest system and a large printer at the side. "A list of my activities is there for you to see and as you'll notice I have visitations on Tuesdays and Wednesdays."

"So I'll be all by my lonesome those two days?" she asked him with an arched brow.

"Do you work on people not liking you? Or is it just an armor you put up?" he asked her mildly.

"But isn't that what you do, Pastor?" she asked him mockingly. "Aren't you supposed to like the unlikeable?"

"Thank you for reminding me of that fact," he told her brusquely. "I am heading out now so I'll see you later." With that he turned and left the office.

Jade sat there after he was gone, one hand going to her forehead wearily. She had been baiting him; daring him to tell her that she was not suitable but he had not taken the bait. She was tired. She had spent so many years just being angry with herself, with God and with her husband about the way her life had turned out and she was just plain tired.

He came back several hours later to find her hard at work. She handed him several messages. "A sister Baker is asking you to call her as soon as you can."

"Thanks," he stood there for a moment, a little hesitant. "Have you eaten?"

Jade glanced at the wall clock and to her surprise she realized that it was way after two. "I am not much of an eater," she told him.

"We can call down to the kitchen and have them send something up," he said.

"What do they have?"

"Today being Tuesday; they have a roast beef sandwich and chicken soup or tuna salad and chicken broth."

"I will go for option one," she gave him a slight smile that had her dimples peeking out. He stared at her his eyes transfixed.

"I'll call and let them know," he told her; before going into his office.

Within minutes an elderly lady bustled in with a tray. "My dear, lovely to meet you!" she beamed; handing Jade her lunch. The girl stared at her puzzled. "Your aunt and I are friends." She clarified. "I hope we will be seeing you in church now." She bustled away before Jade could answer.

Jade found herself eating the sandwich with gusto; it was delicious and the chicken soup was just as good. Before she knew it, she had cleaned off the entire lunch and settled back, drinking the hot chocolate. The day was very cool and even though she had brought along a light sweater, she was feeling a little chilly.

The phone rang just then and putting away her cup, she answered. ""Baptist Ministry, how may I help?"

"This is Sister Baker again, is Pastor John back yet?" The voice sounded a little peeved and Jade's eyebrow rose a little.

"He's back but he's having lunch just now. Let me see if he's available." She put the woman on hold and went inside the office. She had thought about using the intercom but she wanted the woman to stew a little.

"Miss Baker is on the phone again, what should I tell her?" he was reclining against his chair and his lunch was pushed away, half eaten. He looked at her as if he was just noticing that she was standing in front of him.

"I'll take the call thanks," he said dismissively.

Jade shrugged and went back out.

She heard his deep voice murmuring and wondered if the Pastor was eating the forbidden fruit. A cutie like that must have the female members running after him. To each his own, she thought dismissively.

She was so deep into a document she was typing that she did not notice that he was standing at her desk. "Do you need something?" she asked him politely.

"You're a very hard nut to crack aren't you?" he said softly, leaning against the desk.

"I am afraid I don't know what you mean," she continued to type.

"Who hurt you Ms. Reid?" his expression was sober as he stared at her.

"Still don't know what you're talking about," she refused to look at him. Still he sat there, not leaving until Jade was forced to look up at him. "Do you want to delve inside my soul Pastor? To find out what the heck is wrong with me?"

"I think you have been hurt pretty bad and it has affected your outlook on life," he told her softly.

"Well, thanks for your two cent psychology insight, now I am cured." She told him cynically.

"Jesus has a way of working things out," he stood with the intention of moving away. "I am here to talk when you're ready."

"Yeah right," Jade snorted and with a deliberate movement, she turned away from him. He stood there for a while before he left and went back inside his office.

Jade closed her eyes briefly and took a deep breath. The man was getting under her skin.

She finished working at a quarter past five and made a list of the things that needed attention for the next day. He was still in his office so she went to tell him that she was leaving. "Do you need me for anything else?' she asked him politely. He was resting his head back against the headrest of his chair.

"My father left me a legacy and sometimes I am not sure how to handle it," he murmured. Damn. His eyes were so green; you could almost get lost in them.

"I am sure you will," she said noncommittally; chafing to get away.

"Being very diplomatic, aren't you Ms. Reid," he smiled at her slightly.

"I don't know about church happenings so I am steering clear." She answered.

"You're young and very beautiful what are you doing here?" his switch caught her off guard and for a moment she felt herself floundering.

"I have my reasons," she told him coldly; her expression telling him to back off.

"I will find out one of these days," he told her with a wry smile. "Finding out secrets is what I am good at."

"I am sure you have a few secrets yourself Pastor," she told him dryly. "So why don't we keep our secrets to ourselves?"

"I am an open book Ms. Reid, I am a Pastor and I know that Jesus knows our every secret so I am a totally open book."

"Nobody is Pastor," Jade told him with a slight smile. "We all have something we don't want to share."

"Good evening Ms. Reid, see you in the morning." She turned and walked out, not realizing that his eyes followed her out, a thoughtful expression on his face.

*****

When she got home her aunt was in the kitchen and the whole house was pervaded with the smell of baked goods. "So how was it?" Selene glanced at her niece briefly. She was stirring something on the stove and with a sniff Jade realized it was beef stew. On the counter top she saw that there was an apple pie and raisin breads.

"It was good, far better than I expected." Jade put her pocket book on one of the stools and sat on the other one. "Your cooking and baking is making me hungry."

"Good," Selene said in approval. "Get some bowls and let's eat. I came home and felt in the mood to cook and bake and since I am no longer cooking for myself, it is more fun."

Jade got the bowls and took them to her. She had taken off her suit jacket and put it beside her pocket book. "You really like to cook don't you?" she asked in amusement.

"Absolutely," Selene replied with a grin. Jade felt a thug on her heart for the woman who had taken her in when her world had come crashing down. She was not a raving beauty like her sister, Jade's mother, had been but she had a big heart and a serene countenance. "And I intend to fatten you up."

"So you keep saying," Jade said with a smile. They went over to the little dining table and Selene brought over the slices of mouth-watering bread and slices of the apple pie.

Jade spooned up the stew and tasted it; her eyes widening in appreciation as she chewed on the beef and pieces of potato. "This is wonderful," she exclaimed.

"I told you so," Selene grinned, folding the napkin in her lap. "So tell me about work," she urged.

Jade told her what she had done for the day and how much she had actually enjoyed herself. "I had no idea working at a church office would be so exhausting."

"I underestimated it myself dear, until one day I had to sit in for Sister Bailey and then I realized." Selene dabbed her mouth delicately with the napkin. "Suffice it to say, I had to revise my opinion."

They ate in silence for a while. "Aunty why were you never married?" Jade asked curiously.

Selene looked at her niece for a moment and then she gave a small delicate shrug. "I lost the love of my life ten years ago to another woman and after that my heart was never in it again."

"Oh Aunty, I am so sorry," Jade exclaimed.

"Don't be dear," she murmured. "I now live a full and contented life and I no longer pine for him."

"Was he a member of the church?" Jade asked.

"Yes," she nodded. "We had plans to get married and everything but he met someone; younger and prettier and that was that."

"Don't you hate him?"
"I loved him dear and hate and love do not go arm in arm,"

Selene told her. "I hate what he did to us, to me but I could never hate him."

Jade stared at the woman and shook her head. She wished she could be so forgiving. "You're some woman," she said wonderingly.

"Not really," Selene said casually with a smile. "It helps too when you discover that they are now divorced and she has taken him for every penny he had."

"Aunt Selene!" Jade said; her eyes wide and she burst out laughing. "You're bad."

"No, just human," Selene said with a laugh. "I continue to pray for him though and every time he calls I tell him to go take a hike."

"I never knew you had it in you." Jade laughed as she finished her meal; feeling better than she had felt in years. She had a feeling that healing was finally starting.

Chapter 2

She finally gave in. Her aunt has been pestering her for the past two weeks to attend church with her. She had jokingly told her that she is at church every day from Monday to Friday. Her aunt had simply given her an unwavering stare and she had ended up acquiescing. She had sat in the office and listened to Pastor John reading his sermon and making corrections. Things had settled into a routine at the office and Jade had found herself actually enjoying the work she did. He was more out than in and when he was in he was busy dealing with church related business or holed up with the accountant or the steward as they call it.

He had been polite to her and had told her that she was doing a pretty good job. She had also noticed him staring at her a few times but when she looked at him he had looked away.

"Ready?" Selene stood just inside the doorway and looked at her niece. The girl was too beautiful for her own good, she thought, taking in the chic rose pink dress that reached shy of her knees and white shoes with picket thin heels. She had let her hair down and it moved luxuriantly below her shoulders.

"Just about," Jade finished putting the lip gloss on her lips and picked up her small white clutch. "My car or yours?"

"You drive dear," Selene suggested, leading the way downstairs. "I made us some coffee; we usually get something to eat at church, so I don't bother with breakfast. I am so glad that you are coming to church dear, there's no better place to be."

"I am sure," Jade said dryly, heading to the kitchen and pouring her coffee into a to go cup.

"I am certain you are going to enjoy the sermon." Selene said smugly.

They arrived at the church yard at approximately a quarter to eight. There were already several cars parked there and people were milling around saying hi or having conversations. She had come to know a few of the members who had dropped by to see Pastor about one thing or another.

Aunt Selene insisted on her sitting with her at the front of the pew. "I hate sitting in the back don't you?" she whispered. "It seems like you are missing so much."

The service started at exactly eight o'clock and looking around; Jade saw there were a mix of black people and white people and they seem to be in harmony, we have come a long way, she thought in wonder.

Pastor John was casual. He was clearly not a suit and tie pastor; as a matter of fact he was dressed in well-worn jeans and a light pink dress shirt. His blond streaked brown hair was combed back and made him look very young; too young to be standing on the pulpit.

He exude confidence and his strong voice resonated around the building as he spoke about a second chance at life and how God is a God of second chances and he does not write us off, even if people did. As long as we reach out, he will give us a 'do over'. Jade found herself listening in fascination to his words and she was actually interested in what he had to say. She had not been to church in so long that she had forgotten what comfort one can get in just hearing the Word. And he sang. At the end of the sermon, he joined with the choir and sang the closing hymn; his voice was amazing.

"I told you that you would enjoy it," Selene said smugly as they made their way to the auditorium to socialize and eat from the buffet that was spread out on a large table just waiting to be eaten. Her aunt left her at the table to mingle and talk to several members

She was munching on a croissant when he came over. "It's good to see you at church and not in the office." His deep voice unnerved her so much that she jumped a little.

"It was okay," she shrugged nonchalantly; turning to face, man was he handsome. She thought staring into his green eyes.

"Would it kill you to say that you were moved by the sermon?" he asked in amusement.

"I am sure it won't," she flashed him a smile that had him catching his breath. She was much too beautiful for his peace of mind. "You talk a good talk," she tilted her head slightly to look up at him. "But what if you don't believe in second chances?"

"You don't think the fact that you are alive today it is God giving us a chance?" he asked her, picking up an apple and taking a bite.

Jade shrugged, looking away from his mouth. "What do I know, you're the expert."

"I am not, I am simply just learning like the rest of us," he told her soberly. Just then, his attention was caught by a young blonde who was waving at him from the corner of the room.

"Girlfriend?" Jade raised a brow at him, amused to see him looking flustered.

"I am a vessel of God; I don't have girlfriends the way you're implying." He told her stiffly.

"I am not implying anything," she told him cheekily. "But I find myself wondering what a young handsome Pastor like yourself is doing not married to one of these eager young ladies."

"You think I am handsome?" he stared at her, his expression intense. Jade looked away from him.

"I guess you're okay," she shrugged, wishing her aunt would come over so that they could leave. They were actually attracting a number of stares.

"You're something else, you know that?" he asked her softly, forcing her to look at him.

Before she could answer, Aunt Selene came over and she was never happier to see someone. "Aunty," she called out, practically hugging the woman. "Ready?"

"Just a bit dear," she looked at her niece curiously. "Pastor John that was such a moving sermon; you practically had my niece at the edge of her seat."

Jade threw her aunt a pained look and Pastor John said in amusement, "I am glad to know that I was able to move someone. To God be the glory." His gaze shifted as his attention was caught by someone waving to him. "I'll see you two ladies," he said with a smile. "See you tomorrow, Ms. Reid."

They left shortly after and Jade found herself in a contemplatively silence.

"Our Pastor John is a handsome young man isn't he?" Selene said casually. Jade gave her a quick glance; her expression wary. "I suppose he is," she said carelessly.

"A number of young women in the church have been trying to get his attention but with little success." Selene continued.

"Maybe he is gay," Jade commented; although deep down she knew he was far from being gay.

"My dear what a thing to say!" Selene exclaimed just as they pulled up at the gate.

"What? Because a gay minister is something that does not exist?" Jade asked sardonically.

"You are too much of a cynic," Selene said shaking her head; as they made their way inside the house. "I am going to visit a sister in the hospital and I left some lasagna and cold cuts in the fridge and there is also some pumpkin pie and ice cream for dessert."

"Thanks Aunty, you spoil me," Jade gave her a brief hug before bounding up the stairs to change. Selene stood at the bottom of the stairs staring after her, a wistful expression on her homely face. She had been praying every day for her niece to find some happiness and the idea had formed inside her head as she saw her and Pastor John at the food table; maybe there is hope for both of them with each other. With a happy smile she went to change and put on something more convenient for a hospital visit.

*****

She arrived at the office early Monday morning because she had left a document to be typed for a meeting he was having later in the afternoon. He was not there when she arrived and she ignored the little tug of disappointment she felt; telling herself that she was glad he was not there so that she could concentrate on what she had to do.

She was in the middle of making copies of the document when she heard a sound at the door. It was a young girl; blonde with beautiful green eyes and her resemblance to him was so uncanny that Jade did a double take.

"Hi, you must be the new secretary," her voice was soft and very cultured and the suit she was wearing looked like it cost a fortune. "My name is Jenna Wynter-Blake; I am looking for my brother, any idea where he is?"

"No idea whatsoever," Jade told her. So this was the sister; she looked like a beautiful icicle. "I think he went to visit some member or the other. Have you tried his phone?"
"What a novel idea?" the sarcasm was rife in her voice and she gripped her large pocket book impatiently. "I tried his cell phone and he's not answering."

Jade felt her back bristling at the rude comment. "I assure you I am not hiding him in my pocket book so if you called him and you cannot reach him, the best I can do is leave a message and ask him to get back to you." Jade's voice was polite and frigid.

There was silence in the office and both women were so intent on staring each other down that they did not realize that there was a third person in the office; until there was the sound of deep laughter.

"I bet you're not used to being dressed down like that," Pastor John said in amusement coming further into the room. "Jenna, I see you've met our new secretary," He was dressed in his usual jeans and a black dress shirt and he had a laptop bag slung over his shoulders. His hair was mussed by the breeze and he looked young and carefree.

"I have been calling you for ages," she ignored Jade and turned to her brother.

"Ms. Reid, this is my sister," He ignored her and turned to Jade, his eyes twinkling in amusement.

"I've already had the pleasure," Jade told him dryly. She raised a brow as the girl gave her a quelling glance.

"I will be in my office so hold my calls please." He told her; heading towards the office with his sister trailing after him.

"Yes sir," she said smoothly, meeting his gaze head on before he went in and closed the door behind them.

Beautiful siblings, she thought musingly. She had often wondered what it would have been like to have a sibling, someone she could talk to and who would listen to her whining about life.

She was putting away some things for filing when they came back out. Jenna looked as if she had been crying and without a goodbye she sailed towards the door.

"Don't mind her; she is going through a rough patch." Pastor John told Jade, his brow furrowed in concern.

"What happened? Her designer shoes came in the wrong color?" Jade said coolly.

John gave her a level stare and she stared back unabashed. "You don't give an inch do you?" he asked her; his expression forbidding.

"I don't know what you mean. I am sure your sister has genuine problems so I hope you were able to solve them?" she turned back to the documents she had in her hands.

"Ms. Reid – "he began but was interrupted by the ringing of the office phone.
"Baptist Ministry, how may I help you?" she answered sweetly. "He's right here as a matter of fact; please hold." She put the person on hold. "One of your flocks needs your help. Taking it here or in your office?" He gave her a fulminating stare before he turned around and headed back to the office.

Jade shrugged and went back to what she was doing. She called down to the kitchen and ordered up some lunch for him and her as she realized that it was almost one thirty and she still had not come out of his office.

A young bright faced girl came up with the lunch and Jade took the tray from her with a smile of thanks. The door was open so she went in and she saw him reclining against his chair; his expression brooding.

"I am assuming you're not fasting so I ordered something for you to eat," she said brightly. He did not answer so she placed the bowl of soup and chicken sandwich on his desk.

"You're getting under my skin and I can't decide what to do about it yet," he murmured as she moved away from his desk. "You're irreverent and totally unsuitable to be working at a church office."

"Are you firing me?" she asked him; her arms on her hips. She had dressed in pale pink today; the skirt just inches above her knees and had put on a black sweater over the blouse. Her hair was twisted into a neat chignon at the nape of her neck and she had on huge gold earrings.

"Should I?" he challenged her.

"Do whatever you want," she told him and turned around to go out to the office.

"Stop!" he thundered, causing her to jump. "You have no respect for authority and you make me crazy," he told her helplessly.

She turned around slowly, surprised to find him almost in front of her. "You want me to apologize?" she asked him; her heart jumping a little as he came closer to her.

"I want you to stop behaving like a bitch," he told her bluntly and her eyes widened at his use of the word. With a groan he pulled her into his arms, crushing her lips beneath his. After the initial shock, Jade sagged against him, her lips pliant under his. She had only been with one other man in her life and he had taken from her and not given anything of himself, often leaving her dissatisfied and restless but John was stirring up feelings inside her that had lain dormant for years and she found herself responding as his mouth softened beneath hers, his tongue teasing hers. As suddenly as he had started, he stopped, pushing her away from him roughly.

Jade raised trembling fingers to her lips, which were still throbbing from his kiss and they stood there staring at each other, not knowing what to do.

"Forgive me," he said abruptly, raking long fingers through his already disheveled hair.

Without a word, Jade turned around and left the office to go to her desk. It took her several minutes to quell the racing of her pulse and for her body to stop quivering with want. Damn him! She thought angrily. She was doing so well and was getting settled and now he had to come and stir up things; and he being a Pastor to boot. She had just started some filing when he came out of his office. She felt rather than saw when he hesitated beside her desk because she refused to look at him.

"I am leaving for the day," he told her briefly. "Will you please look at me when I am talking to you?"

Jade looked up, her chin held high.

"I am sorry, I was out of line and I can assure you it won't happen again," he told her; his expression guarded.

She gave a regal nod of her head and went back to what she was doing. He stood there for a moment longer as if expecting her to say something then with a weary sigh he left.
Jade waited until she heard him drive out before she let down her guard and with a trembling sigh she put her head into her cupped hands. She just wanted to be left alone. She did not need to be reminded that she was a woman prone to certain feelings; feelings he had stirred up inside her; feelings that she never experienced before. Her husband had told her bluntly the first night they had been together that she did not need to

be satisfied; he was the man and it was her duty to satisfy him.

Her thoughts turned inward as she remembered how loving and sincere he had been until the ring had been on her finger and he had showed her who he really was. She had decided to leave him the night he had had the accident and she remembered the bitter words they had exchanged before he had stormed out of the apartment. She had gotten the call a few hours later about the accident and her first feeling had been relief; followed by regret at the tragic loss of a young life. He had been a bully but she was not sure he had deserved to go like that. She certainly did not need anyone else in her life again – she had had enough of relationships.

*****

Pastor John Wynter the second sat in his car; his gaze unseeing. He had things that needed his attention in the office but he could not stay another minute with her there. Ever since he'd seen her for the first time he had felt the tug of his body. He had kept his body under subjection for the past five years and even more so since he had taken up the role of pastor. He had spent his life being a pastor's son and he had accepted what that meant. Even when he had deliberately gotten out of line, his father had always been forgiving and tolerant with him. His father had never forced him to follow in his footsteps; he had made the decision by himself and he had never regretted it; maybe until now. There had been any number of women who had thrown themselves at him but he had always managed to resist them because he was not interested. His sister Jenna had always been the one to fight tooth and nail to disassociate herself from being a pastor's child. She had gone out of her way to prove that she was not her father's child so much so that she had married a man who's a lawyer that defended shady characters and now she was feeling the burden of her folly.

What a pair, John thought wearily. Maybe if he prayed hard enough, the temptation he faced with Jade in the office would go away. But he doubted it; he was attracted to her and it was not going away anytime soon.

*****

Jade lingered at the office a lot later than five o' clock doing filing and trying to straighten up. She told herself she was not waiting in the hope that he came back; that would be ridiculous but every time the phone rang she hoped it would be him. But he did not call and she finally left, her eyes searching the parking lot looking for his car. It was not there and she told herself she was relieved.

She drove home slowly, admiring the spring flowers along the way. Since she had started working, she had abandoned the idea of planting some flowers but she felt like she would like to now. She needed physical labor to get rid of the surplus energy she had inside her.

Aunt Selene was sitting in front of the television when she got inside; with a jigsaw puzzle in her hands. "Multi-tasking?" Jade asked in amusement; going over to kiss her cheek.

"Nothing good is on; so I've decided to go with the jigsaw puzzle." She smiled in pleasure, pulling down her niece to sit with her. "You look tired; how was your day?"

For a wild moment, she felt like telling her aunt that her precious pastor made a move on her but as soon as the thoughts surfaced; she immediately squelched it. "It was okay," Jade said with a shrug. "I feel like I should do some gardening; the one you interrupted some weeks ago," she said with an impish smile.

"The poor soil," Selene said with a mock groan.

"You'll see Aunty, I'll make us a blue ribbon garden by the time summer comes around," Jade said over her shoulder as she ran up the stairs.

Selene put aside her puzzle and stared at her disappearing figure with a fond smile. It was good to have someone in the house besides her – it was starting to feel like home.

Chapter 3

He did not come Tuesday nor Wednesday. He only called and spoke to her briefly; his voice the epitome of politeness. She was equally polite. Two can play the same game, she thought grimly, punching the keyboard overly hard; her expression solemn.

"I hope I am not the one you're visualizing as you do that." An amused voice drawled at the open doorway. Jade looked up startled, she had been so preoccupied with her thoughts that she had not heard her come in. It was Jenna.

"Your brother is not here and I don't know where he is," She told the woman shortly. She was wearing jeans and a pink cashmere sweater and even her attempt at looking casual failed miserably.

"I know he is not, I spoke to him earlier." She advanced further inside the room; holding out a bag from a fast food restaurant. "I came to ask for forgiveness."
"And you thought you could do so by bringing me food?" Jade asked wryly, not taking the bag immediately. The smell

coming from it reminded her that it was after two and she had not eaten yet.

"Something like that," Jenna gave a delicate shrug; placing the bag on her desk. Her blonde hair was caught in a ponytail and swung every time she moved her head. "I was not myself the other day and I want to apologize."

"It takes someone big to admit that they are wrong and besides I am starving so I would have accepted your apology just to get the food," she told the girl archly reaching for the bag.

"You're different," Jenna cocked her head to one side, studying the girl's face. Jade had chosen to wear black pants and a black and white jacket and white accessories. Her hair was a mass of curls around her face and down to her shoulders. "Not seeking approval like all the others."

"What others?" Jade asked curiously.

"The others who worked in this office and the people who worship in the church who all think that they have to say what we want to hear," Jenna waved a hand languidly. She had taken a seat beside her desk and settled back, making herself comfortable.

"Maybe they feel they have to do that," Jade pointed out, taking a bite of the delicious burger. "I, on the other hand, don't give a rat's ass what you think of me."

Jenna burst out laughing, her green eyes sparkling with mirth. "Told you. Different." She gasped.

"So apart from apologizing and bringing me food what are you doing here?" Jade dabbed her lips with the napkin, staring at the girl curiously.

"I am in the middle of going through a divorce." She said soberly looking away, her expression haunted.

"I am sorry or should I be?" Jade asked her. "Was he a bastard or were you in fact happily married?"

Jenna looked at her startled; then she grinned. "You're the first person who has ever put it like that," she said in amazement.

Jade shrugged. "I don't know all the facts but I firmly believe it is better to be alone than to be with someone who makes you miserable."

"Is that what happened to you?"

"My husband died in a car crash."

"Oh, I am so sorry," Jenna's hand went to her mouth.

"Don't be," Jade told her sharply. "He was a no good bastard."

Jenna stared at her in shock silence. "You don't mince words do you?" she finally spoke.

"If by that you mean that I tell it like it is; yes I do that." Jade said slowly. "It's simpler that way and I do not like hypocrites."

"You are going to do very well in this office," Jenna said with a smile. "Any words of wisdom to someone who is coming out of a ten year marriage?"

"I am not an expert but I would say to you that the best thing is to move on and don't live your life in regrets." Jade told her seriously. "I know it's easier said than done but you have to make a conscious effort. There must be a reason why you have decided to leave so stand by your decision and don't spend your days agonizing over it."

"Thanks," Jenna reached out and grasped her hand. "I feel better than I've felt in days."

"Any kids?"

"No, thank God," Jenna said with a heartfelt sigh. "He kept blaming me for the lack of children but as it turned out it was him all along."

"Children complicate things," Jade agreed. She was beginning to like the girl and found her easy to talk to. She had never been good at making friends but for some reason she felt drawn to Jenna.

"Can we meet for lunch some time?" Jenna asked hesitantly.

"Of course," Jade agreed readily. "Just let me know."

"Thanks – I have shared so much with you and I don't even know your first name." Jenna laughed.

"It's Jade," she smiled.

"Thanks Jade, I am so grateful I could talk to you." Jenna stood, her expensive perfume wafting in the air.

"The good thing is that you won't be leaving the marriage empty handed," Jade told her with a mischievous smile.

Jenna burst out laughing again, "You're right, I will have his money at my disposal. Thanks Jade, I really hope we can be friends." She held out a hand and Jade took it in a firm handshake.

"I hope so too," Jade told her.

The girl left, her pony tail swinging behind her. She turned at the doorway and waved; a smile on her face.

Jade sat there contemplatively after Jenna had left. She had enjoyed talking to her and even if looking at her reminded her of John Wynter; it did not matter. Underneath the sophistication and designer clothes; Jenna was just like any other woman when backed into a corner.

*****

He came in the office early Thursday morning. He had on dark blue dress pants and a light blue shirt. He looked so achingly handsome that Jade had to turn her head away; lest it betrayed what she was feeling. She had found herself thinking about him so much and had to keep reminding herself that he was a Pastor; a vessel of God and therefore he was forbidden.

He stopped at her desk before going into the office. "How are you?" he asked her softly.

"I am doing great thank you for asking." She told him abruptly. She had already put messages and the documents she had typed during his absence, on his desk.

He hesitated by her desk, his eyes seeking hers and then he said, "Deacon Brown is meeting with me shortly so please send him straight in."

"You got it," Jade told him flippantly.

Deacon Brown was a jolly elderly white man who reminded her of the Santa Clauses that you would see at the mall during Christmas. He gave flowers, some white lilies that he told her he had picked at his garden before coming over. "And you thought of me or am I the first woman you saw coming in?" Jade asked with a twinkle in her large brown eyes.

"You have wounded me, dear lady," he told her with a sorrowful expression on his ruddy face. "I picked them especially for you."

"Then I am flattered," she told him cheekily as she indicated for him to go right in.

She was kept very busy for the afternoon. He had given her a proposal to prepare because as he had told her they wanted to expand the soup kitchen and start serving breakfast and lunches not only to the homeless but also as school feeding program for the various schools and he was looking for sponsors.

Jade found that she was very interested in the venture and decided that she wanted to be a part of the committee.

She was packing up to leave at five thirty when he called for her to come into his office. "You're very efficient and I want to tell you that you are doing a very good job." He told her as soon as she entered. He was reclining against the chair, his head resting on the back. He looked weary, Jade thought.

"Thanks," she told him coolly. "Anything else?"

"My sister said she spoke with you at length today," he continued ignoring her abrupt attitude. "Thanks for being friendly to her."

"You don't have to thank me," Jade told him off handedly. "I kind of like her."

He laughed in amusement. "Would you mind sitting for a minute?" he asked her.

She sat on one of the chairs in front of his desk.

"My mother died a few years before my Dad and it has been just Jenna and me," he began folding his hands together as he stared at nothing in particular. "We grew up with the expectation that we were supposed to be better than the average kids because our father was a pastor. It was a lot of pressure on us and we were watched every second of the day. Jenna hated it and she did everything to show to everyone including our parents that she was going to live her life different. I hated difficulty so I was satisfied to just toe the line." He paused for a while and Jade sat there not saying anything, waiting for him to go on.

"She went ahead and got involved with a man who was totally unsuitable just to spite our parents. It broke my mother's heart and my father ignored her; never reaching out to embrace her husband. So I guess she is paying the price now."

"We fight for individuality," Jade commented. "We want to prove that we are our own person and in doing so we often end up taking the wrong path but we can always come back from that path as long as we identify that we made a wrong turn. It's never too late."

"I thought you didn't believe in second chances," he said in amusement.

"I never said I do not believe in second chances and besides, you have convinced me that God gives us a do over when we get it wrong," she looked at him curiously. "Your sister with all her bravado is scared and needs guidance; you need to be there for her."

"I am trying to be; not as a pastor but as her brother." He told her softly.

"Do you like this?" she waved her hand at the office. "Do you like being at the beck and call of others? Hearing their problems? Trying to be there for them?"

"It can be a burden sometimes but I love being able to do God's work." He said simply.

"What about your problems?" Jade persisted. "Who do you go to?"
"We all go to the same place Jade," She looked up startled as he said her name. "What about you? Where do you go to?"

"I keep them bottled up inside," she said bluntly. "Telling people your problems only give them something to talk about and you end up with the problems unsolved."

"What happened Jade?" he asked her softly. "Who hurt you so bad that you approach life like it is a war zone?"

"People happened," she told him coolly, standing up with the intention of leaving. "People tend to disappoint you and let you down."

"What about those who care about you?" he had stood up with her and came from around his desk; moving closer to her.

Jade felt the warning bells going off inside her head but she stood her ground.

"What about love?" he whispered. He was near enough to reach out and touch her and even though he just stood there, Jade felt the heat rising from his body.

"What about it?" she asked huskily, berating herself for her lack of control.

"Don't you want to know what it feels like to love and be loved?" He reached out and lifted her chin to look into her eyes; his green ones smoldering with hidden fire.

She shook her head unable to utter a word. She wanted to feel him; she wanted him to touch her and she wanted to touch him back.

He pulled her towards him slowly as if giving her a chance to back away but she didn't and he pulled her up against him. "I have been thinking about you a lot. You have invaded my thoughts and I can't get you out of my head." He murmured against her mouth. "Tell me to stop," he said huskily.

She couldn't. She did not want him to. He bent his head and took her mouth with his. With a sigh Jade sank into his arms, her hands resting against his chest as she opened her mouth to welcome his. With a groan he pulled her closer, deepening the kiss, his arms tightening around her waist. Jade felt her body tingling. She had never felt this way before. With her husband it had been quick and no measure of satisfaction but this was so different. It was as if her body had come alive. She found herself reaching up to put her hands around his neck, molding her body to his in total surrender.

John felt her breasts pressing against him; her nipples hard against his shirt and he wanted to take her then and there. He wanted her, needed her and he could not stop. It was a sound out in the parking lot that had them separating. He pushed her away from him, sagging back against the desk, his body shaking.

Jade felt bereft; her body one long nerve ending as she struggled to come terms with what he made her feel.

"I am a pastor," he muttered, combing agitated fingers through his thick hair. "I can't do this."

Taking a deep breath, Jade stepped back. "I get it, Pastors are not supposed to have sexual feelings."

He stared at her for a minute and then he laughed shakily. "Go home Jade, please," he told her softly. "I can't think when you're here and I need to think."

With a shrug Jade turned to leave; then she hesitated. "Are you going to apologize?"

"I can't because as you said before you don't like hypocrites and I would be one if I told you I am sorry and I am not." He said softly.

With a small smile Jade said, "Good," before she headed towards her office. She automatically tidied up her desk and picking up her pocket book before she left.

Theirs were the only two cars in the parking lot and Jade sat in her car for several minutes thinking about him. She wanted so much to go back in there and pick up where they had left off but she knew how dangerous that would be.

When she got home her aunt was outside in the garden digging in the soil. "What are you doing?" Jade asked as soon as she got out of the car. It was already dark out and also a little nippy but the outside light was on.

"Getting ready for summer," Selene said with a grin.

"When I said it, you thought I was going crazy so what's wrong with this picture?" Jade put her pocket book on the porch and slipped out of her shoes; walking on the velvety grass in her pantyhose.

"I decided you were right so I went to the flower shop to pick up some plants." Selene told her; her attention on carefully putting a small rose bush inside the hole she had dug. "Care to join me?" she looked up at her niece with a smile.

"Oh heck, why not," Jade flung up her hands in surrender. "Just give me a minute to get out of these clothes and into something more yard worthy." She hurried inside and up to her room to change into sweat pants and an old sweat shirt and slipped into a pair of sneakers.

"So, how was work?" Selene asked her passing her a trowel.

"It was okay," Jade said casually, her mind flashing back to the heated moment she and Pastor John had spent inside his office, her body trembling in remembrance.

"I am glad you're enjoying your job dear," Selene said in approval.
You have no idea, Jade thought dryly, digging furiously.

"Watch it honey, gentle does it." Her aunt said, placing a hand on hers.

They stayed out there for an hour and then went inside to shower and eat in the kitchen. Her aunt had made turkey sandwiches and chicken soup and Jade found that her appetite had opened up with the worked she had done in the garden.

"I met Jenna," she said casually, sipping the soup appreciatively.

"Poor Jenna," Selene shook her head sadly. "Such a misguided young lady. I hear she's on the verge of being divorced."

"Have you ever met him?" Jade asked curiously.

"Yes, I have. They had been to church a couple of times and I have to say that I really thought they would last. Very sad when a marriage does not work out." Selene said with a sigh.

"What was their father like Aunty?" Jade put down her spoon and gave her aunt her full attention.

"A very solid and loyal man." Selene said fondly. "He was a very good Pastor; always ready to listen to your problems no matter how busy he was. His wife was a little standoffish though; even though she tried to be the supportive Pastor's wife; you could always see that she wished she was anywhere but at church. John takes after him and I think he's doing such a good job."

Jade insisted on doing the washing up after they had finished eating and shortly after they retired to their bedrooms.

She could not sleep. She kept feeling his lips on hers, his tongue inside her mouth and the fire he had created inside her belly. She had no idea what she was going to do about him; about what he made her feel but she knew she wanted to feel him on her, inside her. She knew it was wrong but she could not help herself.

Michael had told her in no uncertain terms that he had married her because she looked good on his arm. He was going places and one could not go places with an ugly woman beside them. The woman had to look good. He had shattered her dreams and ideals and made her feel like a possession instead of a person. She had stopped trying to win his respect and the little love she'd had for him had fled out the matrimonial window long before he had been killed.

He had insisted that she stopped working and stayed home. He was an up and coming lawyer and it did not look good that his wife was a mere secretary – it did not matter to him that 'the mere secretary' was part of a huge corporation. She had tried to stand up to him but he had been a first class bully and had taken a belt to her naked bottom, leaving welts that had been there for months. He had cut her off from her friends and had kept her isolated. Jade had settled into a state of euphoria where nothing could reach her.

She had gone to functions with him and smiled dutifully and he had gotten off when other men stared at her. Whenever that happened he had come home and pushed her down on the bed; ripping her clothes off, driving himself inside her until he was satisfied and then he would get up and go take a shower.

She had gotten married too soon, falling for a man that was suave and handsome on the outside but a total piece of crap on the inside. She was not about to make that mistake again. Pastor John Wynter stirred up feeling she had thought were dead and buried, he made her feel alive and excited and she wanted to explore that. She had a high sense of right and wrong and she had a great deal of respect for God but for the first time in a long while she was feeling again and she did not want to deny herself of it. She had no intention of making the mistake of falling in love with a pastor; she had every intention of guarding her heart. She was not going to make the same mistake twice. But she could not stop thinking about him; he had gotten to her with just a kiss and she wanted to feel more of him. She needed him.

Chapter 4

She went to church that Sunday. He had avoided her the whole time on Friday by popping in and out of the office; never staying long enough for them to have a conversation. Jenna had called and asked her out to lunch but she had been backed up so she had told her another day.

She had dressed carefully for church. The weather was unseasonably warm with a slight breeze so she put on a black and white horizontal striped dress with a small cap sleeves and flared from the waist down; her small waist was cinched with a tiny red belt. She wore red shoes and clutch and her hair was caught up in a red jeweled clip.

"You look amazing," Aunt Selene told her looking over the girl in speculation. "Any reason why you're looking so fancy?"
"I am going to church and it's a beautiful day, so why not?" Jade returned her stare blandly.

"I see," Aunt Selene held her gaze for a while then turned to pick up a thin white sweater to put on over her red and white dress. "I am driving my car dear; I have some people to visit after church."

They arrived just as it reached eight o'clock. Aunt Selene went in ahead of her with some friends and she went in and sat near the aisle. He was not preaching today but he was seated on the pulpit; in his usual jeans and dress shirt but it was Deacon Brown who was taking the service. She felt rather than saw when he looked at her but she refused to look at him. She wanted to concentrate on the sermon and he was too much of a distraction.

Deacon Brown, although not as charismatic as Pastor John, held his own. He spoke about the woman who had the issue of blood for twelve years and how her healing had come at a time when she had given up on the physicians she had been going to over the years. He spoke about the healing power of Jesus and that no matter what one is facing in life; there is no limit to what the Great Physician can do.

Jade found herself listening attentively and she thought reflectively of how much she had gone through over the years. She went to the breakfast room right after and grabbed a plate and a glass of orange juice and headed to the office. She had been hoping to catch a glimpse of Jenna but to her disappointment the girl was not there. I have to give her a call, Jenna decided. A few members had called out to her and several of them had stopped to chat and for the first time in her life, Jade felt as if she belonged somewhere. This wasn't so bad after all; she smiled to herself as she placed the full plate on her desk along with the juice. She had left something undone on Friday and since Aunt Selene was not going home right now she thought she would catch up on some work.

She was busy going through the filing cabinet having kicked off her shoes and her head buried in the filing cabinet when she heard his voice. "I wondered where you had gotten to," he said softly.

Jade stiffened. She had been looking forward to seeing him and wondered how she would react when she did. She turned around slowly. He was lounging in the doorway; his hands in his pockets. "I had something to do that could not wait until tomorrow."

"Your commitment to the job needs to be lauded." He came further inside; unnerving her with his nearness.

"Duly noted," she looked up at him. Without her heels, she was way in the disadvantage, barely reaching his shoulders. "Took a day off from preaching?"

"I was struggling with something, so I asked Deacon Brown to take the service." He gave her a long slow stare, leaving her in no doubt as to what he was struggling with. "Besides he is a trained minister."

"You've been avoiding me," Jade commented. She wanted to reach out and trace his lips but was afraid of starting something that neither of them could control.

"I saw you come in and was going to leave you alone but for some reason I could not," he murmured. He reached out a hand and lifted her chin. "You're beautiful and I am in deep trouble." He laughed ruefully. "I have been doing a lot of praying and a lot of good it has done for me."

"Maybe you should continue praying," she murmured huskily, her tongue snaking out to wet her lip. He groaned; his eyes mesmerized as he stared at the movement.

"What are you doing to me Jade?" he asked, his voice tortured.

"I suppose the same thing you're doing to me," she whispered. She pulled away from him and went to close and lock the door. "I don't want us to be interrupted." She told him as she came back to where he was standing, staring at her.

She stepped into the circle of his arms and he closed his hands around her waist. "God forgive me," he said achingly, his mouth zeroing in on her lips which were opened and waiting for him. Jade felt the feelings rushing through her body and she whimpered inside his mouth with the enormity of it. One of his hands came up and cupped her head with stunning force; holding her steady as his tongue delved deep inside her mouth. With a muffled groan, he tore his lips from hers, his breathing ragged. "I need you Jade. Please I can't hold out much longer." His green eyes smoldered with what he was feeling.

"I haven't been with anyone since my husband died," she told him huskily; her eyes holding his. "I want it to be you."

"Not here," he told her hoarsely. "Come with me to the cottage."

The church yard was empty by then and because the building was isolated there was no one around. The cottage was charming and old fashioned and the living room was strewn with gaily colored straw mats on the board floor.

"I tried to stay away from you," he murmured, pulling her back into his arms as soon as they reached inside. "But I kept thinking about you, about the way you smell; the way you walk and the way you talk." He took her lips with his, his mouth hungry and demanding. She responded boldly, wrapping her arms tightly around his neck.

This time it was she who pulled away. "I want to see your bedroom," she told him huskily, taking him by the hand.

With a hoarse laugh he pulled her with him to the bedroom nearest to the living room. It was large and airy and very tidy and the king sized bed dominated the room. He stood there looking at her, not moving; not saying anything. Jade took the initiative and without a word, she reached around and slide down the zipper of her dress, stepping out of it to reveal the sheer white panties and matching bra she had on. She knew what her body looked like and she knew without prejudice how good she looked; her husband had forced her to realize what an asset she had. Without any shame whatsoever she unhooked the bra and slipped it off; her bare breasts firm and the nipples already hardened.

Still he stood there as if rooted to the spot. She walked over to him and unbuttoned his shirt using her hands to push it off his body. His chest was muscled and had smatterings of blond hair. Bending her head her lips closed over one of his nipples. With a groan he dug his fingers into her thick hair, his teeth clenched as she tongued his nipple thoroughly. When she started on the next one his control slipped and with a hoarse cry he lifted her and placed her on the bed. Hastily pulling off his pants and underwear he climbed back on the bed.

"My turn now," he told her urgently; sliding a hand between her legs; his fingers slipping between her panties. She was already wet and his eyes bore into hers as his fingers slid in and started moving gently at first then urgently. Jade cried out. The feeling foreign to her; she felt as if she was on the edge of a precipice poising to jump. He bent his head and took a nipple inside his mouth, pulling on it, his teeth grazing; his tongue softening what his teeth had done.

"John," she whispered; digging her fingers in his hair. He brought her up and over; his fingers ruthless as she rode out the storm, his name on her lips.

He rose and knelt above her, suspended for a moment; his penis was throbbing and Jade found herself staring at it in fascination. She had only been with one other man and Michael had been wanting down there even though he had pretended that he was full of sexual prowess. John was much larger and for a fearful moment Jade wondered if she could accommodate him. "I won't hurt you," he told her hoarsely as if reading her thoughts. With that he gently penetrated her, his teeth closing over his lip as her tightness closed over him like a vice. He stayed still inside her, his forehead resting against hers. "I have never felt this way before," he told her, his voice strained. "I have never met anyone like you Jade and I don't know what to do." The last part ended in a tortured whisper as he moved inside her. His mouth closed over hers and Jade wrapped her legs around his waist; opening herself more to him; lost in his lovemaking; her body quivering with the feelings assailing her. Never in her wildest dreams had she ever known it would be like this and she wanted the feeling to continue.

John lifted her hips and plunged into her, his body giving her everything. He was almost delirious with the pleasure he was feeling and he knew he was in deep trouble.

They came together tumultuously; their cries mingling in the room; their bodies quivering with the force of the orgasm that rocked them. He kissed her; deepening the kiss as she moved restlessly underneath him and even though he had spilled his load inside her; he still could not let go. Maybe he feared that he would have to give her up; so he kissed her; his mouth fused to hers, his body moving over hers slowly. He wanted her to stay; what happened after this, he refused to think about; this was here and now and right now he knew he wanted her to be his.

He released her lips finally but still he could not pull out of her; his body was reluctant to do so. He wanted to stay like this for the rest of his life. "I'm not hurting you am I?" he whispered.

"If I say yes are you going to get off me?" Jade asked saucily. She loved feeling him on top of her and her hands were still buried in his hair.

"I would do so reluctantly," he told her tenderly. "Jade I –"

"Don't say it," she told him hastily.

"Say what?" he asked puzzled, lifting his head to look at her.

"Tell me how you feel." She told him. "I am attracted to you and you make me feel so alive and different and I have never felt the feelings you stir up inside me and I want to feel them over and over again." She took a deep breath. "You are a Pastor for goodness sake, and you are not going to be satisfied with a roll in the hay."

He stiffened over her. "Is that what I am?" he asked angrily. "A roll in the hay?"

"No, and that is the problem," she told him bluntly with a sigh. "I was married before and it was awful and I don't see myself repeating that mistake. I love the way you make me feel and I am satisfied with just being with you this way but I have a feeling that won't cut it for you."

He rolled off her and sat on the edge of the bed. "I won't be satisfied with that," he agreed. He stood up and pulled on his pants. "I want more," he told her; sitting on the bed and trailing his hand up her thigh; coming dangerously close to her pubic area. "I want more of you and I am patient." His fingers feathered over her; rubbing her genitals. "I'll make you want more," he told her softly and with a deliberate move he slipped two fingers inside her, rotating them slowly; watching her eyes cloud over and her lips parted as her breath escaped rapidly. "I need more," he worked his fingers inside her swiftly never stopping until he brought her to her peak; her cry anguished as she closed her legs around his fingers. He pulled them out slowly, giving her time to stop trembling and to her amazement he put them inside his mouth; his eyes on hers as he licked his fingers clean. With a groan he pulled her up and against him, crushing her mouth with his. Jade went weak as she tasted herself in his mouth and with a tortured groan she gave in to his passion. He pulled down his zipper and pulling her to the edge of the bed he plunged inside her; his hands pulling her legs to his shoulder as he took her hard and fast; his hands holding her hips steady. Jade gripped the sheets as she ground her body against his; her cries echoing with his as they reached their peak. He pulled out of her in the middle of his orgasm and spilled his seed on her stomach, his body shaking with the enormity of his passion.

He lifted her and took her into the bathroom where he bathed her off gently, his fingers lingering on her breasts and her pubic area. Then he dried her off with a large fluffy towel and dressed her. The entire time Jade remained silent. She had never been treated like this and she was not sure what to do about it.

"Confused aren't you?" he asked her wryly as he hooked her bra in place. "You don't know what to think or what to say. What started out being just sexual attraction for you is starting to feel like something else, am I wrong?"

"Stop trying to analyze me," she told him impatiently, turning around while he zipped her up. It was almost five o'clock and she knew her aunt was probably wondering where she was.

"I am not giving up Jade," he told her softly, spinning her around.
"Suit yourself," she tried to sound off hand but it came out sounding hoarse. "I have to go."

"I know," he told her huskily. "But not before this," he murmured, kissing her lips softly, his mouth moving over hers until she opened her mouth and her tongue met his. It was he who broke off the kiss and they were both fighting for control.

Without a word, she fled from his bedroom and did not stop running until she was in her car. The place was still deserted and Jade rested her head on the steering wheel fighting for control. Her hands were still trembling and she still felt the imprint of his penis inside her.

He was right. She had never felt anything like what he made her feel and she had never met anybody like him. She had not wanted to leave. She switched on the engine and backed out of the yard before she could change her mind.

Her aunt was there when she got home and was in the kitchen making a salad. Jade had sat outside in the car making sure she looked the same as when she had left for church. She was not ready to deal with questions yet. It was too soon.

"Hi, where have you been?" Aunt Selene placed a bowl with the salad on the table. There were already a bowl with steaming white rice and another one with what looked like pork with carrots on top.

"I stayed at the office to catch up on something," Jade said flippantly. The food reminded her that she was starving; she had not had time to finish the breakfast she had taken at church. "I'll just go and change and come and join you." She said quickly, hurrying up the stairs to change out of her dress.

She stared at herself in the mirror. Her lips were slightly swollen and putting a hand to her mouth she closed her eyes as she remembered what it felt like to feel his mouth on hers. It was amazing. She sat down on the edge of the bed; her legs weak with the feelings assailing her. She knew she was not supposed to be thinking about him but she could not help herself; he had exceeded her wildest expectations.

"Are you coming?" her aunt called up.

Jade snapped out of her reverie and hurriedly pulled on a T-shirt and a pair of shorts. "Sorry to keep you waiting," she mumbled, pulling out a chair. Aunt Selene was already seated around the table.

"Will you say Grace my dear?" Aunt Selene asked reaching out a hand for hers.

Jade looked at her startled and closing her eyes she began: "Heavenly Father, the giver of life and the provider of what we have; please accept our humble thanks for this that you have once again provided. Amen."

"Amen" Aunt Selene uttered with a beaming smile. "Thanks dear."

Aunt Selene told her about one of the ladies she had gone to visit. "Poor dear she is so upbeat and cheerful even though we could see that she was in a great deal of pain." She said shaking her head. "Sometimes we have so many things to give thanks for and yet we complain."

"What's wrong with her?" Jade asked curiously, tasting and swallowing the soft and tasty pork in appreciation.

"Final stages of breast cancer," Selene shook her head. "The doctor has given up on her."

"But as we heard from the sermon today with the woman suffering for twelve years from the issue of blood that God works in mysterious ways and it is not over until He says so." Jade reminded her.

"My dear how intuitive!" Selene squeezed her hand enthusiastically. "We should have brought you with us to remind us of the sermon that was preached this morning. We are on the 'sick and shut in' committee at church and we have visitations every other Sunday and sometimes during the week."

"Does it help?" Jade wondered, reaching for the salad bowl.

"Immensely," Selene said at once. "People tend to get lonely during times of trials and tribulations and they like to know that there is someone who will look out for them even if we cannot do anything but pray."

"I suppose," Jade said with a shrug. She had gone through her own trials and tribulations and had borne it herself because she had been too ashamed to tell anyone that her husband had been abusing her.

Jade washed up while her aunt went into the living room to watch some religious program. She went straight up to her room, claiming exhaustion and the need to prepare for work the next day.

He called her as she was brushing the tangle out of her hair. "You left your earrings here, am I to assume it's because you have every intention of coming back?" His deep voice in her ear made her feel weak.

"Maybe," she told him, putting the brush aside and heading over to the bed.

"What are you doing now?" he asked her softly.

"Seriously?" Jade asked mockingly. "Are we going to be doing that now? Asking mundane questions like two teenagers?"

He laughed softly. "What am I going to do with you Jade?"

"You know what you can do with me John," Jade told him mildly, a reluctant smile on her face.

"I miss you," he told her softly. "I am here trying to put together a proposal for the soup kitchen and all I keep seeing is your face."

"I just left there John," Jade reminded him; not for the life of her would she admit to him that she missed him too.

"Sure you can't come over?" he asked huskily.

"Really? What will people say if they saw me sneaking out of your house in the middle of the night?" Jade asked him mockingly.

"They would probably say that the Pastor is falling in love," he told her huskily.

Jade went silent and her heartbeat quickened.

"You are obviously suffering from lack of sleep." She told him coolly.

"How long are you going to run away from that fact Jade?"

"Goodnight John," she told him hanging up the phone hastily.

He had no right to say that to her – no right at all.

Chapter 5

She dressed carefully for work the next morning with him in mind. The suit was navy blue and she had on a white silk blouse underneath. She was still contemplating cutting her heavy tresses but she had to admit that she liked his fingers through it. She could not believe that she was dressing to impress a man; especially a man of the cloth. She must be going crazy. It had finally happened; she had gone off her rockers.

Aunt Selene was on her way out the door when she came downstairs. "I have an early staff meeting dear," she slung her pocket book over her shoulder and picked up her car keys. "Oatmeal's on the stove. Eat something," she ordered as she closed the door behind her.

It was half past eight and Jade ate a little bit of the oatmeal, pouring coffee into her to go cup to take with her.

When she got to the office he was already there waiting for her in the outer office. "I have to go and see someone," he told her as soon as she came in. He was dressed in jeans and a T-shirt and his hair looked teased; possibly by the slight wind blowing outside. "I wanted to see you before I left." Without warning he swept her into his arms, crushing her lips with his. Jade welcomed it and opened her mouth to take in his tongue, her breathing quickening. Neither of them was conscious of the fact that someone might come in through the open door. His mouth moved over hers gently, his arms tightening around her waist. He let her go slowly, his breathing rapid and his erection evident.

Jade reached down and touched him, squeezing gently and rubbing her hand over him. He groaned as if in pain and he moved against her wanting desperately to pull it out and put it inside her right then and there. "Jade," he said hoarsely. She pulled down the zipper and reached inside, her hand closing on the warm flesh, stroking and caressing. He closed his eyes and let her handle him. Then he pulled away from her, zipping up his pants and putting distance between them. "You're killing me," he told her tightly, his face tense.

She stepped over to him and kissed him on the lips softly. "Ditto," she murmured, leaving him to go to her desk.

With a muttered oath he left hurriedly. She hoped he did not meet any of his congregants on the way out to the car.

Jenna called her and invited her out to lunch. John still had not come back and had called to tell her that he was running a little behind schedule but he would be there sometime soon.

She left as soon as he came in at a quarter to one. "I am off to lunch." She told him as soon as he came into the office.

"My sister is parked outside, is that who you're going to lunch with?" he asked her curiously. He looked so boyishly handsome that she wanted to chuck lunch with his sister and have hot delicious sex with him.

"That would be right," she grinned at him. "You look tired; want me to call and get you something to eat?" she asked him.

"I ate something on the way," he said dismissively. "Why are you going to lunch with my sister?"

"I am going to eat because I have been offered a free lunch and people generally don't say no to something that is free." Jade told him blandly. "What are you afraid of?"

"Nothing," he shook his head as if to clear it. "Enjoy your lunch."

"I intend to," Jade told him cheekily; leaving him standing there staring after her.

Jenna's car was frivolous and obviously expensive. It was red and the top was down even though it was a cool enough day. Jade went around to the passenger side and sat down enjoying the cool feel of the upholstery of the bucket seat. "I thought my brother was keeping you chained to the desk," Jenna said flashing her a smile as she put the car into drive. She was wearing a pink silk blouse and a cashmere sweater over it with white pants. Her hair was in a ponytail.

"Not quite," Jade said with an answering smile. "Nice car."

"Isn't it though," Jenna caressed the steering wheel with one hand. "A present from my cheating husband for my birthday last year."

"Almost makes you want to stay married," Jade said dryly.

Jenna burst out laughing. "Not quite."

They had lunch in a swanky new restaurant in town. Jade found herself looking around and admiring the ambiance. There was a fountain in the middle and the lunch time chatter was subdued along with the clinks of utensils on china ware. They had the chef's salad and steak and Jenna had champagne while Jade had a fruit cocktail.

"I got married on a whim," Jenna mused, sipping her champagne delicately, her green eyes darting to and fro as if looking for someone. "I wanted to upset my parents' apple cart. I wanted to show them that I was nothing like them; I was not 'holy' and 'righteous'; I just wanted to show them I was my own person."

"And I am sure you showed them," Jade said in amusement.

Jenna laughed softly. "Boy did I!" she shook her head. "I like you Jade. You are not like my so called friends who just tell me what they think I want to hear or who kept telling me to look the other way because Barry, even though he was cheating on me with everyone who wore a skirt, was a very good provider."

"My husband beat me in the worst possible way and when he was not beating me, he was humiliating me; making me felt as if I was stupid and I was damned lucky to be married to him." Jade sipped her drink to quench her parched throat. She had never told anyone this before and she could not understand why she was telling this girl that she had just met. "I was planning to leave him when he died and as much as I worked on feeling guilty and sorry that he had died, I could not. So now I live by the motto: 'Me first, everyone else after'. Don't let anyone make you feel less than you are and don't stay where you're not comfortable."

"I had no idea," Jenna stared at the beautiful black girl in amazement and wonder. Barry had never laid a hand on her; he was smart enough not to be so foolish because of her brother and her dad being a Pastor and she had told him that if he ever did she would wait until he was sleeping and she would find the dullest knife in the kitchen and hack off his penis. That had done it.

"No one did," Jade shrugged. She wanted to change the subject. "So what are you getting in the divorce settlement?"

"A lovely six bedroom four bathrooms house on top of the hill complete with an outdoor swimming pool and a tennis court," Jenna grinned. "Unfortunately, I have no intention of staying in it. It's way too big for one person and I don't want a reminder of Barry in my life. I have bought a two bedroom townhouse and I will be moving there shortly."

"Why don't you turn it into a summer camp for the kids at church?" Jade suggested, leaning forward, a sudden sparkle in her large dark eyes.

"You want me to use my totally beautiful house for kids at church to wreck it?" Jenna asked incredulously, looking at her as if she had gone crazy.

"It would be supervised by adults and it's just for the summer and then you can use it for when the church is having their retreat at different times during the year. It can also be used when they are having pastoral seminars three times for the year."

Jenna stared at her wordlessly and then she burst out laughing. "Did my brother put you up to this?" she demanded.

"You know better than that," Jade told her coolly. "It's just a suggestion, you can think about it."

"Would you like to see it?" Jenna asked suddenly; a twinkle in her eyes.

"What?"

"Would you like to see the house?"

"I guess so," Jade said uncertainly.

"Great," Jenna said with satisfaction. "Come over tomorrow night and spend the night with me. We'll have a girl's night and drink booze and talk about bad marriages."

"I don't do girl talk," Jade warned her.

"Okay, so we will drink booze and watch a movie or two and you can leave there and go to work." Jenna persisted.

"Okay fine," Jade said with a slow smile.

"Great, so that's settled." She gave the waitress her card to settle the lunch bill. Jade glanced at her watch and realized that it was minutes to three.

They left shortly after and got to the office in record time. "I am glad I met you Jade," Jenna leaned over and gave her a kiss on the cheek. "I have a feeling we are going to be best friends."

Jade smiled and climbed out of the car; waving to the girl as she drove out of the parking lot. John was waiting for her in her office when she got in.

"I'm sorry I'm late," she told him contritely; rushing past him to put her pocket book on her desk. "Your sister is a bad influence. What do you need?" She had booted up her computer and her hands were poised over the keyboard.

"How was lunch?" he asked her. He was leaning against the desk and he was staring at her broodingly.

"It was good; we went to that swanky new restaurant and the food was incredible." She told him. "You okay?"

"No, I am not." He said shortly. "I can't concentrate Jade, I can't do anything without thinking about you and meanwhile you go about your way as if everything is okay. How do you do it?"

Jade pushed back her chair and looked at him. "I do it because I have a job to do and I cannot let my body control my every move."
"What happened to you?" he asked her softly.

"John, I am not going to discuss my life with you, not now. We are in a church office and any moment one of your congregants can come in and hear us so I suggest you pull yourself together and go about the Lord's work." Jade said coolly.

"I told you I am falling in love with you and you have not said a word," he told her harshly. "What type of person are you?"

"A normal person," she told him stiffly, her eyes blazing. "A person who suffered abuse from her husband for years and a person who will never let that happen to her again." Her voice had risen and she calmed down with an effort. "Leave me alone John and let me get some work done. You don't know me enough to fall in love with me."

He strode over and closed the door and came around her desk, pulling her up and onto him. "I am sorry that your husband was not man enough to know that hitting women was not acceptable and right." He told her through clenched teeth. "And if he was still alive, I would kill him with my bare hands. But I am telling you what I feel about you, so please don't belittle it." His mouth came down on hers with bruising force, his tongue forcing its way inside her mouth. Jade moaned and opened her mouth to receive him hungrily, returning his kisses with fervor. He pulled away from her, his breathing ragged. She sank back into her chair and he came from around her desk. "I am falling in love with you so deal with it." He told her stonily as he went back to open the door and left the office.

Jade sat there trembling, one hand on her lips still bruised and swollen from his crushing kiss. She sagged against the chair and closed her eyes; fighting for control. He was stripping away her defense piece by piece and she was not sure if she liked it one bit.

*****

He called her that evening after she went home. He had come back into the office but there had been a meeting of sorts which had lasted until after five so she had left after poking her head inside to ask if there was anything he needed before she left. He had looked at her for a moment; his expression telling before he had told her no and that she should have a good night. She had smiled at the other people in the room; closed the door and left.

"Tell me what happened to you," he said urgently, his voice deep and disturbing.

"Who's this?" she asked, pretending that she had not recognized his voice. Her aunt had gone to visit some friend so she was alone at home and was trying to watch some comedy that was not appealing to her.

"Don't play games with me Jade," he said impatiently. "What did he do to you?"

"I don't want to discuss it with you," she told him.

"I want to hear, Jade and if you don't tell me now I am coming straight over there and damn the consequences." He told her shortly.

"You actually said damn," Jade said in wonder. "Am I being a bad influence on you Pastor Wynter?" she asked mockingly.

"Cut it out Jade, I am serious."

"He was physically and emotionally abusive and he made me feel like nothing. I was arm candy for him and behind closed doors he treated me like crap." Jade said tonelessly. "I swore to myself when he died that no man will ever do that to me again."

He was silent and Jade could hear him breathing. "He hurt you and I cannot bear it; I want to lash out at someone, something."

"It's not your problem," Jade said nonchalantly although her heart skipped inside her chest. It felt good to have him defending her like that.

"Stop it!" he said crossly. "I know you don't want to hear it but what affects you, affects me and I am not going to hide what I am feeling. I want to see you."

"You saw me today," she told him huskily "And you'll be seeing me tomorrow."
"Jade, I want to feel you, taste you, be inside you," his voice had dropped an octave and Jade felt as if she was dissolving like a gelatin. "Don't push me away baby, I need you so much."

"John, please," she whispered huskily. "Stop doing this to us; you know what is at stake and I don't want to be the one to destroy your calling. I am not getting married again and I know you will want nothing less."

"I am not giving up," he told her huskily. "I refuse to give up so you just have to deal with it."

Jade was silent for a moment as if absorbing what he said to her. "I am having a sleep over at your sister's house tomorrow night." She told him, more to change the subject than anything else.

"You are?" his tone was one of uncertainty.

"Yes, she wants me to see the place and want us to drink booze and talk about bad marriages and what jerks men are." Jade told him facetiously.

"Not all men," he murmured. "Are you going to tell her about us?"

"There is no 'us' John and I certainly am not going to tell your sister that her Pastor brother plunged his penis inside me over and over again until I thought I was on the moon." She told him impatiently.

"That's how I made you feel?" he asked her softly.

"John, I am hanging up now," she warned. She had not meant to tell him that and she was a little peeved at herself.

"I need you Jade and I would never hurt you," he told her softly. "I will be thinking about you tonight as I do all the other nights. Tell me you'll be thinking about me too."

"I will be thinking about you," she told him reluctantly.

"Was that so hard?" he said huskily

"Yes, it was," she answered. "Good night John."

"Good night baby," he whispered huskily.

Jade hung up the phone and turned the television off. She had only been half watching it anyway. He was right; he was getting to her so much that her every thought was about him. She felt his body on hers at various times and she wanted him again. She had never felt this way about anyone before and the feeling was new to her. She was afraid of opening her heart to him and he turned out to be, if not like Michael but he ended up disappointing her and causing her pain. She was afraid to love; not that she had loved Michael and that was what made her feel like a hypocrite. He had looked damned good and she had been so flattered that he had taken such an interest in her and she had allowed herself to be swept off her feet. What she was starting to feel for John was not half of what she had felt for Michael.

*****

The object of her thoughts was sitting in the living room in the dark. He was struggling with his feelings and at first, he had tried to pray but the words had not come; would not come. He had told Jade the truth. He had never met anyone like her and he had never felt this way before in his life. He had been happy to just be the person who gave comfort and imparted the word to others and when he had been asked over and over again by his associates about settling down he had laughed and said that he was married to the work he was doing for God. He knew there were several single women who were just waiting for him to show the slightest bit of interest but he had always kept them at a distance; he was not interested. But now, Jade had popped into his life and had turned it upside down with her frankness and unorthodox way of speaking and doing things and the way she behaved as if she did not give a damn about what people thought of her.

She had captured his heart and even his sister could not stop talking about her. What was it about her that made them slaves for her feelings? He wondered in despair. Jenna had called and told him that Jade was coming over and she sounded so much better; she sounded as if she was starting to live again and he had been speaking to her for so many months and had not been able to get through to her but in two short meetings Jade had done far more for her than he had ever done. What was it about her?

He combed his fingers through his hair. He needed her in his life and he did not know what to do about it. He had no idea what the church body would say about him wanting her to be his wife but first he had to convince her that he was different from that bastard she had been married to before.

He stood up and went into the kitchen to brew some tea. His mother had often told him that there was nothing that could not be solved with a pot of tea. He strongly doubted it but he did not drink hard liquor so a cup of tea would have to do. He missed his mother and wished she were alive so she could give him some much needed advice. He had not been very close to his father; who had dedicated his life more to the needs of the church than to his own family but he had always respected him.

He sipped the tea contemplatively and with a decisive move he went up to his bedroom; the bedroom that still smelled of her; the bed that still had her imprint on it and the pillow that had locks of her dark hair and pulled it towards him; a smile on his face. He was not giving up on her; no matter what she said.

Chapter 6

The house was breathtaking. The view was spectacular; you could see all around and there was a small lake running around the back. Jade had arrived at work early and John had called her and told her that he had some people to visit. He came back in the afternoon and had meetings until she was ready to leave. She could see the disappointment on his face as she told him she was leaving for the day; she knew he wanted to say something personal to her and he wanted to touch her because she wanted to do the same.

Jenna was waiting for her outside and she followed behind her in her car.

"My God, I can't believe you don't want to live here anymore." Jade exclaimed as soon as they had parked on the paved driveway and alighted. "I wouldn't want to leave." There were towering palm trees on either side of the long curving driveway and there was a water fountain in the middle of the yard.

The house was made of cobbled stones that had turned a smooth gray and the door leading into the living room was a massive tan oak.

"Welcome to my palace," Jenna grinned, taking Jade's overnight bag and leading the way up the curving staircase. She put Jade into the guest bedroom; a pale pink with a huge queen sized bed and matching dresser and armoire. There were white rugs strewn over the shiny board floor. "The bathroom is through there," she indicated a door off the side of the room. "Too bad it's too cold out for the pool but another time. I'll be in the living room with the liquor," she said with a grin leaving Jade to change.

Jade sat on the bed; her eyes taking in the luxurious room in wonder. How the other half lives, she thought wryly. She quickly changed into jeans shorts and a T-shirt and put on the fluffy white bed slippers she saw at the foot of the bed and headed downstairs. She ran her hand along the curving staircase, enjoying the feel of it.

"It makes you want to slide down it, don't you think?" Jenna asked in amusement staring up at her. She had changed into silk pajamas and was barefoot.

"Ever tried it?" Jade asked her with an answering smile as she joined her in the living room.

"Once and nearly popped my ass in the process," Jenna said with a laugh. "Never tried it again." She handed Jade a glass of wine and sat down on the white wraparound sofa indicating that Jade did the same.

"What do you think of my brother?" Jenna asked unexpectedly.

"What?" Jade looked at her startled, the glass halfway to her lips.

"He's sweet on you," Jenna was watching her closely and Jade had to work hard at schooling her features.

"Don't be ridiculous!" She said sharply. "Not only is he my employer, but he is also a Pastor."

"And he's quite good-looking and he has blood running through his veins." Jenna counteracted smoothly, placing her wine glass on the small glass top table next to her. "He has been quizzing me about you. What we spoke about and he hoped that I had not said anything to upset you. My brother has not shown the slightest bit of interest to any of those fluff pieces in his congregation but the minute you show up you have him all over the place."

"I have no idea what you're talking about," Jade said airily, gulping down the wine too fast and gasped as her throat contracted.

"Liar liar pants on fire," Jenna said softly, looking at the girl in amusement. "I thought we were going to dish about men."

"We were going to dish about bad marriages and men who are jerks and your brother is off limits." Jade said firmly.

"He works too hard," Jenna continued as if she had not heard anything. "He is trying to prove to our dead father that he is not going to fail and you would be good for him. You are different and beautiful and you pretend that you are tough but you are not so much."
"I had no idea you were in the matchmaking business," Jade casually.

"Just only for my brother and what is becoming my best friend," Jenna told her frankly. Her green eyes were direct and Jade was hard put not to look away from them; they looked so much like John's that she felt the felt the need for him piercing through her. "You're attracted to him and you're fighting it."

"A matchmaker and a psychic," Jade curled her feet under her.

"Okay fine," Jenna threw up her hands in defeat. "I'll just sit here and pretend that you and my brother are not hot for each other and we will talk about something else."

"Good," Jade told her mildly. "Because talking about your brother's sexual proclivities or lack thereof is totally weird."

"To be continued," Jenna warned. "How about some pizza?" she asked, reaching for the phone.

"That sounds delightful." Jade agreed, totally relieved that the girl had dropped the subject. Sister or not, she wasn't comfortable discussing John with anyone right now.

They had a great time chatting and laughing. Jenna was well read and to Jade's surprise she had a degree in English Literature. "I am not a total airhead you know," she said at Jade's startled look.

"I didn't think you were," Jade told her soberly.

Jenna told her about growing up in the church cottage and how their father had wielded a very strict hand saying over and over again that the family had to be perfect because it was the way of the Lord and 'what would people think if they saw us doing this or that', Jenna shook her head wryly. "My mom put up with a lot from him and was always careful never to cross him. I don't know if that was what totally screwed me up and prevent me from forming healthy relationships."

"At some point we have to stop blaming the people in our lives for the way our life turns out," Jade said contemplatively. "Easier said than done actually, because although I keep telling myself that it's because of me why I have decided not to get married again; he was the one who ruined it for me and it's as if he's reaching from the grave to control my life and I keep asking myself: 'What am I doing about it?'"

"I know you do not want to hear this but you're saying the same thing I was saying to a few minutes ago Jade." Jenna leaned forward earnestly. "Are you going to let him stand in the way of what might be the love of a lifetime?"

Jade sat there in silence for a while. Jenna was right, for two years she had allowed Michael to control her emotions and holding herself aloof from the possibility of being with someone else.

"I am still not talking about your brother, "she told the girl firmly. "Not right now," she added softly.

Jenna looked at her in understanding and then nodded.

They chatted until way into the night before Jenna suggested giving her the grand tour before going off to bed. The house was the epitome of luxury and the kitchen had every modern appliance there was. "Totally wasted on me because I do not cook," Jenna said wryly.

They ended up in the huge master bedroom where the room was dominated by an enormous king sized bed that was on a dais. The room was very feminine and to Jade's surprise there was no sign of a man ever having being an occupant.

"I got rid of all signs of him," Jenna said answering her unspoken question. "He took his entire clothing etc. and I got rid of the rest. I spent so many wasted years with him Jade and the sad thing is I did not love him."

"I understand," Jade said sympathetically. They were laying on the huge bed and Jade felt herself enjoying the comfort of the soft eider down pillows. "I could get used to this," she told Jenna with a smile.

"Feel free to come over anytime," Jenna told her. "Me casa es su casa'"

They both fell asleep right there, Jade never bothering to go into the bedroom assigned to her.

Her phone alarm woke her up the next morning and by the time she had come from the bathroom and put on her clothes for work; Jenna met her downstairs with coffee and bagel. "Thanks," Jade said in surprise, climbing on the padded stool in front of the marble top counter. "I didn't know that socialites wake this early." She added teasingly, sipping the excellent coffee appreciatively.

"Some socialites don't, I do," Jenna said airily as she sipped her coffee. "Besides, I have a nine o'clock meeting with the lawyer."

"You'll be okay," Jade told her reassuringly as she picked up her stuff with the intention of leaving. It was a quarter to eight and she wanted to reach work before eight thirty.

"Thanks Jade," Jenna hugged her fiercely and after a slight hesitation Jade returned the embrace. "For everything."

She got to the office at eight fifteen and he was not there yet. Jade ignored the pang of disappointment she felt and went straight to her desk to start her work. He came in minutes after nine and he looked tired and sad. "What's wrong?" she asked in concern.

"A church member just died at the hospital a few minutes ago and I have to go and pray with the family," he told her; raking long fingers through his burnished brown hair.

"I'm sorry," she murmured sympathetically.

"How was your sleep over?" he asked her with a faint smile.

"It was very good," she told him with a smile. "I fell in love with the house."

"I wish you would fall in love with me," he said soberly, staring at her. "I want to kiss you," he added huskily.

"John-" she began.

"Don't say anything Jade," he told her holding up a hand. "I am in a very bad place right now and I need you." He went over and closed the door, leaning against it his eyes on her.

"Come here," he said softly.

Jade stood up on unsteady feet and made her way towards him. She was wearing a red wool dress that molded her figure lovingly, outlining her delicate and subtle curves and her hair was in an elegant chignon at the nape of her neck. His arms closed around her causing her to gasp.

"I wanted to kiss you so badly yesterday but I couldn't and then I wanted to call you but I was not sure you would appreciate me calling you when you were at my sister's," he told her huskily, his mouth kissing her cheek. "All these rules, when all I want to do is be with you." He groaned, reaching for her lips with his. Jade opened her mouth for his kiss, her hands reaching up and around his neck, her body molding to his. He sighed raggedly as he took her tongue and gently pulled it inside his mouth. Jade felt the emotions coursing through her and moved her body against his restlessly.

"John." She murmured against his lips; her hands sliding into his hair.

"I need you," he told her hoarsely. "And I cannot go on like this; you're torturing me Jade. You're breaking me," he whispered agonizingly, crushing her lips with his; his mouth moving over hers in a desperation that had her caught up inside it. "I love you," he dragged his mouth away from hers, his green eyes blazing with raw emotions. "I love you."

Jade stiffened in his arms and made to pull away but he would not let her. "I am not letting you go," he told her huskily. "I want to marry you Jade." She pulled away more forcibly this time and he let her go.

"You're unfair," she told him heatedly, crossing her arms over her heaving bosom. Her insides were mush and she was not certain she could stand for much longer.

"Why?" he demanded.
"Because you wait until I am vulnerable before springing that on me." She accused him.

"You mean the fact that I am in love with you and want you to be my wife?" he asked dryly, shoving hands into the pockets of his dark gray pants. "Most women would jump at that and say a quick yes but not you Jade, oh no, that is beneath you."

"How dare you!" she was trembling with fury this time. "You think that a proposal and those three little words would have me over the moon? How desperate do you think I am?"

Before she was finished, she knew she had said the wrong thing. His face had turned to stone and his eyes had cooled distinctly. Jade wanted to apologize and tell him she was wrong but she remained mute.

"I am sorry, I have offended you and it won't happen again," he told her coldly. With that he turned and pulled the door open and left. She stood there after he had left her expression stricken. She had done the very thing she had told Jenna that she would not do; she had let what had happened between her and Michael screw up what was happening between she and John.

And yes, she admitted to herself slowly; she was falling in love with him and she had denied it and was fighting it every step of the way. She slowly went to her desk and sank into the chair. She had turned him away and she knew he wouldn't be saying anything like that to her again.

She went about her duty automatically. Sister Bailey came in and chatted with her briefly and Jade knew she said all the right things because the woman left beaming. He did not call nor did he come back to the office and she found herself looking up every time she heard footsteps outside the office

Page 109

hoping that it would be him but he did not turn up. She lingered in the office after hours hoping that he would turn up and tell her that he understood and then she would explain to him why she had been such a bitch but she left there without hearing from him and seeing him. Jenna called her and gave her an update of what happened at the lawyer's and Jade almost told her what had transpired between her brother and her but she resisted the urge.

She drove slowly home. Her aunt had called her to let her know that she was preparing something for her but she was not hungry.

She got to the house and her aunt was still in the kitchen. The smell of baking pervaded the air and she reluctantly went into the kitchen.

"I hope you're hungry my dear," Selene said cheerfully as she set the table. "I am going to need to hear all about your night with Jenna."

Without warning she burst into tears. Selene stood there for a moment in shock and then she hurried over to her niece, gathering her up in her arms.

She gently led her to the living room and they sat, Jenna's head buried in her lap and Selene stroking her hair gently. She waited patiently while the girl recovered her composure.

Jade sat up a little embarrassed; wiping her face with a handkerchief her aunt passed her. "I did something awful," she said sadly.

"I am sure it's not as bad as it seems dear," Selene said reassuringly.

"It is," Jade insisted. "I have broken his heart and I now realize that I am in love with him."

"And who are we talking about dear?"

Jade turned and looked at her aunt. "I am talking about John," she said with a sigh. "Pastor John."

"I see," Selene said not in the least bit surprised.

"You don't seem surprised." Jade commented, looking at her aunt curiously.

"I am not," Selene said, clasping her hands before her. "I saw the signs dear but I waited for you to realize them yourself. I never asked you to give me details about what went on between you and Michael but I realize that you have been hurt pretty badly."

"He made my life a living hell," Jade stared off into space. She told her aunt most of what went on in her marriage. Selene sat there in silence and listened horrified as her niece unfolded the secrets of her sham of a marriage.

"My dear," she murmured, reaching for her hands and holding on to her gently. "I am so sorry that you had to go through all that but it's behind you now and you need to look at the future and stop living in the past. Don't let him control your life; or you are making him win."

"I have been telling myself that every day and I think it's just sinking in now," Jade said sadly. "You haven't said anything about Pastor John."

"He's a lovely young man and he has not shown the slightest interest in any of the young ladies that have been throwing themselves at him ever since he came of age and some of the older ones too," Selene said with a smile. "You'll make a fine wife for a Pastor; you're just what he needs."

"So Jenna told me," Jade said with a pleased smile. "He's not talking to me though."

"What! The Pastor not speaking to you!" Selene's eyes twinkled. "You have to make the move dear and let him know how you feel." She hugged her suddenly in delight. "I am so happy for you and Pastor John! My prayers have been answered and He has provided a good man for you."

"Thanks Aunt Selene," she said soberly. "I just hope it's not too late."

She went to bed that night feeling better, even though she had not heard from him but she was feeling as if it was going to work out. She guessed she could always tell him that she was pregnant, she thought wryly. She suddenly realized that she wanted the works with him. Marriage and kids and whatever it took to be to be a Pastor's wife.

Her phone rang as she was drifting off to sleep. It was Jenna.

"What have you done to my brother?" she demanded.

"What are you talking about?" Jade asked her heart jumping.

"He came over and was going on and on about wanting to give up the ministry because without 'her' nothing is worth it." Jenna told her impatiently.

"It's not your affair Jenna," Jade told her bluntly.

"Oh no you don't," she said heatedly. "You don't get to play that card with me anymore Jade. You are my best friend but John happens to be my brother."

"Where is he?" she asked subdued.

"He's upstairs in bed trying to sleep off a whole bottle of wine and the thing is Jade, my brother does not drink. He does not have the tolerance for it."

"I will see him tomorrow Jenna," she told her friend. "I am sorry I can't discuss it with you now until I have spoken to him."

"Are you going to make it better or worse?" she demanded. "Hopefully better," Jade told her.

"Good," she said curtly and hung up the phone.

Great! Jade thought, she had managed to alienate both brother and sister. Could this day get any worse? She wondered despairingly.

She could not sleep so she got up and took out a Bible she had seen in the drawer in the side table beside her bed and she started leafing through the thin pages looking for some words of comfort. She came upon Matthew 11: vs. 28 "Come to me, all you that are weary and are carrying heavy burdens and I will give you rest."

Jade hugged the words to her and for the first time in a long time she knelt beside her bed and prayed. "God, I have not been close to you for a long time. I have been angry and afraid and I have not spoken to you because I have been so buried in self-pity. I need you now Lord and I don't know how to find my way back." She hesitated a fraction. "I also pray for John and ask for your guidance in our lives as we deal with this that you have thrown our way. Amen."

To her immense surprise she slept right through the night.

Chapter 7

"You told your sister that you want to give up the ministry because we had a disagreement?" she attacked him as soon as he came into the office. She had thought of running to him and apologizing and letting him know that she had fallen in love with him too but when she woke up this morning she had decided against it. She was not going to let any man, no matter who he was, use emotional blackmail on her and she had no intention of starting their relationship like that. She had reached work early this morning; dressed to kill in emerald green pants suit and black stilettos. He came in at half past nine looking like hell and she had been sitting there stewing and waiting to pounce on him.

"I don't want to talk right now," he told her coolly, heading for his office. His clothes looked like he had slept in them.

"Well that's too damned bad because I want to talk," she told him heatedly, getting up from her chair and following him inside the office. He went and sat behind his desk.
"Please Jade, I have a headache and I don't want to talk." He said wearily.

"You expect me to feel sorry for you because you resort to drinking because you had a problem?" she asked him, her arms akimbo. "You are a Pastor for crying out loud and you're supposed to be an example. What if one of the people who you preached the word to Sunday after Sunday come in here and see you like this?"

"Then they would know that their Pastor is a human being and is capable of having problems just like them," he told her through clenched teeth.

"I am so disappointed in you John," Jade told him with a shake of her head; a surge of satisfaction going through her as his head snapped up and his eyes blazed.

"You're disappointed in me?" his voice had gone dangerously soft.

"I am disappointed in you as a man and as a Pastor," she went on stubbornly, holding his gaze.

"Well, we can't have that can we?" his voice was still soft but there was a hint of steel behind it. He stood up and came towards her slowly. For a fleeting minute, Jade wondered if she had gone too far but she stood her ground. He passed her and went to lock the door.

"What are you doing?" she squeaked as he came back towards her backing her up against the desk.

"You have been a thorn in my flesh since the first day I met you," he told her harshly reaching out to pull her against him forcibly. "I have put up with your irreverent speech and your habit of talking first and thinking later but this time you have gone too far," his voice had dropped and so had his head. Jade pushed against him ineffectually.

"John let me go," she said coolly. "You're not in a good frame of mind."

"Really?" he whispered against her lip. "I assure you I am in the right frame of mind." He took her lips with his hungrily; his lips moving over hers restlessly; his hands like steel bands around her waist. Jade had to grab his shirt for leverage as her knees weakened. The kiss deepened and softened and what started out as an angry assault on his part turned into something else. Jade felt her arms going around his neck, cradling him as she returned the kiss with equal fervor. He pushed her back until she was half sitting on the desk, as he bent her over backwards his tongue deep inside her mouth, his chest grazing her breasts which were by now painfully hard.

He pulled away from her slowly and Jade released him reluctantly; every nerve ending in her body quivering. "What do you think of me as a man now?" he asked her huskily, moving away from her.

She got off the desk and straightened her clothes. He was looking a lot better, more animated. Definitely not looking as if his dog or his best friend had died and even though she was aching for him she was satisfied with the result. She came close to him and combed her fingers through his hair and then she wiped the lip gloss from his lips. "Now you look like the man I am in love with," she told him softly stepping back and hurrying towards the door to open it.

She looked back and he was rooted to the spot and she left him there with a smile on her face. Let him stew on that, she thought smugly.

He came out while she was on the phone with a church member who wanted to know if there was going to be fasting service today. "I am not sure Sister Pryce but Pastor John is right here, let me ask him," she put the lady on hold and looked up at him innocently. "Sister Pryce wants to know if there will be fasting service today."

He stared at her as if he could not believe what she was asking. "Tell her to call back or you'll call her back, I don't give a damn," he said impatiently, looking as if he wanted to strangle her.

Jade released the hold button, "Sister Pryce, Pastor John is a little uncertain right now. He is going to check and call you right back." She listened for a few more minutes and laughed at something she said. "I will let him know that. You have a blessed day Sister Pryce." She put the phone back in the cradle. "Sister Pryce said to tell you that she hopes you are getting some rest."

"I don't care," he started to raise his voice and Jade could see him trying to relax. "You told me you love me and then waltz out here and expect it to be business as usual. Jade, I don't know if I am coming or going where you are concerned."

"Oh, you wanted me to wait until we are at a more convenient place for me to tell you?" she asked him casually. "How about your place tonight? I don't cook so we will order take out or if you want to cook that's fine by me and before and during our lovemaking and even afterwards I will tell you that I am in love with you and although I am a little scared of being a Pastor's wife; or any wife for that matter, I really don't want to spend the rest of my life without you. Does that suit you?"

He stared at her in shock, his mouth partially open. "You're impossible!" he retorted, spinning around and heading for the door.

"So how about seven tonight?" she asked his retreating back, fighting back the smile.

He did not answer but continued to walk. Jade was just starting to type up a document when he came back in and stood in front of her desk. "You love me?" he asked huskily, his green eyes smoldering and suddenly it hit her with a force that left her breathless. She loved him so much that she could hardly breathe.

"I love you," she told him, every sign of flippancy gone from her tone. They stared at each other and just as she was about to come around to him the phone rang again.

"Later," he told her softly; turning away to leave.

Jade took a deep breath and answered the phone brightly; the trembling still inside her.

Jenna called her during the course of the day. John was still out but he had called in to check up on her.

"You better not change your mind about later," he warned her.

"Why would I?" she had asked him airily.

"So how is it between you and my brother?" The girl demanded.

"And good day to you too," Jade said dryly.

"Good day, how is it between you too?" She said impatiently.

"It's none of your business," Jade told her firmly.

"Jade, if I have to come to the office and squeeze the information from you, so help me God, I will," the girl threatened.

"For children of religious parents you and your brother can be very demanding," Jade said mildly.

"Jade-" Jenna began.

"Okay, calm down. We are having dinner at his place later. Does he cook; because I don't," Jade told her.

The girl squealed and Jade had to move the phone away from her ear. "I am coming over right now. Oh my goodness, I demand to be maid of honor or technically is it matron of honor and we can have the reception at the house; there is a lovely gazebo at the side."

"You're not coming over because I am working and I have no intention of letting you plan my wedding. You've gone ahead of yourself; we have not talked about marriage yet." Jade told the girl firmly.

"But you will," Jenna said equally firmly. "I will buy the dress, my treat and I know this lovely woman who does outstanding wedding cakes; she owes me a favor."

Jade burst out laughing. "Jenna, I have work to do so I am going to hang up now."

"Okay fine." Jenna said with a laugh. "Oh Jade, I am so happy it's you. We are going to be family!" she squealed.

"I am hanging up before I go deaf," Jade said with a grimace.

"Okay, I will talk to you later," she said hastily. "Oh no, not later; you guys will be busy. Oh and Jade, he cooks very well and he enjoys doing it, so unlike me."

Jade was still smiling after she hung up the phone.

She called her aunt at about five thirty to let her know that she will be home very late. "I take it things are sorted out?" she asked mildly.

"We're in the process of doing that," Jade assured her.

"Do I hear wedding bells then?"

"You're as bad as Jenna," Jade laughed. "Let us at least talk about it first before you guys start planning it." She paused and then said. "Thanks Aunty."

"For what dear?" Selene asked genuinely puzzled.

"Thanks for being there for me," Jade told her.

"No place would I rather be," Selene told her fondly.

John came back to the office about six and there was a healthy glow on his cheeks. "I am going to the office to make a phone call and then I will be going over to the cottage to start dinner." He told her. "Should I expect you around seven or earlier?"

"Maybe earlier," she told him. She knew he was being cautious and she loved him for it but she wished he would come around and put his tongue down her throat. Soon enough, she decided. "I can't wait to run my hands up and down your penis and possibly even take it inside my mouth." She told him blandly.

He stood there staring at her; his green eyes wide.

"I have on a black lace teddy and I want you to undress me slowly," she continued. "Okay, run along now and make your call I will see you later." But he did not move and Jade looked up at him with an innocent smile.

"Jade," his voice was hoarse and his erection was evident. Before he could say anything else, the telephone rang and Jade saw him walk slowly into his office.

She was still on the phone when he left and she stayed at the office for several more minutes making sure that she had finished putting together the proposal for the soup kitchen before she shut down her computer and tidied up her desk.

The parking lot was empty except for her car and she made her way over to the cottage. He was in the kitchen and he had changed into a white T-shirt and well washed jeans and he was barefoot.

"Something smells good, what is it?" His kitchen was nice and warm and homely. "Beef stew," he answered turning to face her. She had taken off her shoes and jacket and left them in the living room.

"Your sister and my aunt are ready to plan our wedding," she told him coming closer to him and standing on tiptoe to wrap her arms around his neck. She touched her lips to his and he opened his mouth to taste her. "I have been longing to do this since this afternoon." She murmured, catching his bottom lip between her teeth causing him to shudder.

"Jade," he said hoarsely.

"Hmm," she was busy running her tongue over his lip.

"You're making me crazy," he told her huskily.

"We wouldn't want that would we?" she told him sweetly capturing his tongue with hers. He gave in with a shudder and deepened the kiss.

"Take me upstairs," she told him huskily, tearing her mouth from his.

"The food?" his tone was thick and uncertain.

"Later," she told him urgently.

Without another word, he turned off the fire under the stew and picking her in his arms, he headed for the bedroom.

He placed her gently on the floor; keeping her near him. "There is going to be a wedding?" he asked her softly. He could not stop touching her as if he wanted to believe that she was really there.

"Isn't there?" Jade pulled his shirt over his head. She wanted to touch him.

"I want to marry you," he told her; gasping as she ran feather like fingers over his nipple. "I can't think when you do that," he muttered.

"I don't want you to think," she told him bending her head to take the nipple between her teeth. He was lost. With shudder he held on to her. She did not stop there. She unhooked his jeans and pulled down the zipper, reaching inside his underwear for the warmth of his penis. John's knees buckled and he blindly reached behind him to feel for the bed dragging himself and her and leaning against it. She got on her knees and took him inside her mouth; closing her lips around him. John gripped the bed tightly his head thrown back as he fought for control. He was trying hard to stay focus as she destroyed every last vestige of control he had; her mouth moving up and down him, slowly at first and then urgently.

He could not take it anymore. With a tortured groan he dragged her up and buried his fingers into her hair; resting his forehead against hers; his breathing harsh. "I love you," he told her achingly. With a hoarse cry he crushed her lips with his; his movement hurried and hungry as he plunged his tongue inside her mouth.

Jade matched him move for move; giving every part of her. He released her only to take off her clothes, his eyes flaring at the provocative teddy that molded itself to her curves. "You're so beautiful," he murmured, running his hand over her breasts; lingering on the nipples. He kicked off his jeans and took off his underwear and lifting her, he placed her gently on top of the bed. He knelt there looking at her; then he reached down and sucked a nipple through the black lace. Jade gasped and arched her back as he pulled the nipple between his teeth. He ventured down and when she made as if to take off the underwear he stopped her. His lips made their way down to her pubic area where he licked her there causing her to jump. He closed his mouth over her and sucked her through the sheer material. Jade cried out; her hips bucking. He held her still and continued and then reaching his fingers through the material he parted the lips of her vagina and gently entered her with his fingers. Jade was almost hysterical with the passion flooding through her. He took her over and beyond; his fingers working furiously as she cried out her total surrender. He did not stop, even when her cries had quiet down to mere whimpers her body trembling. He peeled off her teddy and his eyes traveled the length of her body; his expression stormy. Then without a word he came over her and entered her gently; staying still as her tightness closed over him.

"I will never hurt you, physically or otherwise," he told her huskily. "I can't hurt you Jade and I will never control you. You still have not told me what he did to you exactly but I will wait and I promise you that I will always be there for you."

"I know," she told him softly, reaching up to bury her fingers in his hair. "Now, would you please make love to me?"

He needed no further bidding as he started moving inside her, slowly at first and then when she moved with him he increased the pace, capturing her lips with his. He came before her; he had been trying so hard to wait for her but his control broke and he could not hold out much longer as he spilled his seed inside her, his cries hoarse. Jade held him to her gently and by the time he was finished it was her turn and wrapping her legs around his waist she brought him closer to her; her head thrown back as she called out his name over and over again.

He switched position and pulled her on top of him, gently stroking her bottom. He was still inside her and every now and then he would move his hips causing a pleasant sensation inside her.

"Can we talk now?" he asked her softly. She was lying against his chest and a feeling of contentment settled over her.

She nodded her head.

"I don't want you to leave," he told her ruefully and Jade smiled as his voice rumbled against her ear. "But I am a Pastor and there are certain rules I have to adhere to, so I am saying that to say that I want us to get married as soon as possible."

Jade lifted her head and looked at him in amusement. "Are you going to propose to me properly?"

"Jade," he began then sighed. "I am going to have a very interesting time being married to you aren't I?"

"Most definitely," she told him cheekily, planting a tender kiss on his lips. "But you're going to love it."

They talked. She told him about the painful events in her marriage and the time she had spent picking up the pieces of her life. She felt him stiffened beneath her and she knew he was hurting for her. She kissed away the tenseness from his mouth and continued to talk about her mother whom she had been close to and how she had felt when she had died.

He told her about his childhood and how he had tried to be a good kid; one that measured up to his father's standards and how he had felt compelled to take over a ministry that he had been groomed to take over.

"I went through the motion for a while Jade, and then I found out that my heart was in it and I was not just doing it because my father had left his legacy to me. I want to take that legacy and make it mine." He told her soberly.

"I think you have already done that," she told him softly.

He smiled at her gently, tucking a strand of hair behind her ear. "Being a Pastor's wife is not going to be easy," he told her with a hint of uncertainty.

"I am going to be your wife and loving you makes it a lot easier," she told him flippantly.

"How soon?" he asked her huskily.

"As soon as humanly possible. I want this as much as you do." She told him gently.

"I have never met anyone like you and I don't know what I did to deserve this but I am thanking God for that." He murmured, reaching up to take her lips with his.

They did not speak for a while as the kiss continued and he hardened inside her. Jade moved her hips slowly and he moved with her; his hands reaching downwards to hold her hips in place while he lifted himself slightly to reach her. She brought her knees up and breaking off the kiss she sat on him grinding her hips against him; her hands curled on his chest, her eyes holding his. He held onto her slim hips and watched as her eyes glazed over as she rode him furiously, her breath coming in short pants. With a hoarse cry he sat up and she wrapped her legs around his back as he plunged upwards into her burying himself deep within her.

They came furiously, clinging together as the wave washed over them; their cries mingling together as their mouths fused to celebrate the emotions running like wild fire between them.

He held her for a long time; not wanting to let her go and Jade held on to him; her eyes shimmering with tears. She had met the love of her life and she was where she belonged.

Chapter 8

There was a general air of excitement at church that Sunday. Their dear Pastor was getting married and to that lovely girl that works in the office. It was like a fairy tale and a miracle all rolled in one. There were of course some disappointed sisters who had set their caps at him and had known him for a very long time and had hoped when he decided to settle down it would be one of them. But nonetheless, after the sighs of regret and a few tears shed, they decided to be happy for them. After all it was God's will wasn't it? And who are they to interfere with the will of God. A number of the elderly ladies wondered if she would fit in – not just because of the color of her skin surely because they had a lot of members who were black and both black and white got along well together. No, they saw that she was beautiful and sophisticated and the way she dressed and also the way she talked like she did not give a hoot about what people had to say after she had finished speaking. But they saw the way their Pastor was around her; he looked at her with love in his eyes and he was always holding onto her.

The wedding was set for the next four weeks and everyone wanted to play his or her part. They also wondered what ministry she would be a part of. Sister Bailey gently suggested that she take over the women's ministry because Sister Adams was getting on in age. Jade firmly declined, telling the pushy woman that when the time came she would make her own decision and that she did not think it's very Christian to take away something from someone just because they were getting on in age. The woman was properly chastened and went away to tell another sister that the woman that Pastor was marrying was not very accommodating.

John had given her a diamond solitaire on Saturday even though she had told him that she did not need an engagement ring but he had insisted; he wanted her to get the works. They had argued about the office because John had told her that when they got married she was not going to be working there anymore; there would be too many things to occupy her time as his wife. He had finally persuaded her that it would not look good for the Pastor's wife to be working in the office and she had told him heatedly with her arms on her hips. "Fine. But I get to choose my replacement because if I feel like screwing my husband in the middle of the day I will jolly well do so."

He had stared at her wordlessly for a moment and then she had burst out laughing. "You should see the look on your face," she told him, her eyes twinkling. "I will make sure and lock the door first before I climb in your chair and sit on you."

"You're impossible," he told her ruefully pulling her into his arms. "And I love you so much that sometimes I don't know where you end and I begin. I don't know what you're going to say from one minute to the next and I find myself wondering how I ever did without you."

"Now you no longer have to wonder," she told him softly. They had managed to escape the throng of well-wishers and the talk of wedding plans and escaped to the office. Announcing their engagement meant they had to be discreet because they were going to be watched and even though they wanted to go over to the cottage, they had to stay away until they were sure they were alone.

"Usually I say to couples who announce that they want to get married to make sure that the person they are with is someone they will want to spend the rest of their lives with even on a bad day." He murmured. She was still in his arms and had kicked off her olive high heeled shoes that matched the dress she had worn and she had to look up at him. He was dressed in dark blue pants and a white shirt and his hair was

www.SaucyRomanceBooks.com/RomanceBooks

combed back from his face, the gold highlight glinting in the light from the office. "I tell them that marriage is supposed to be a commitment that should be held by both parties and the only third party should be God." He released the pins that held her hair on top of her head and watched as the heavy black curls tumbled around her face. "I love you so much my baby, and no matter what you say or do that will never change, do you believe that?"

"I believe that," she told him softly, her eyes shimmering with tears. He made her feel so special it was like he made up for the bad breaks she'd had in her life. "I love you too, very much and even though I tried to fight it; I couldn't." She reached up and touched her lips to his. "I told myself there was no way I was ever going to get married again not after what I had been through but funny how things turn out." Her tongue reached out and touched his lip.

John captured her tongue between his teeth and Jade felt the jolt straight through her body. He kissed her; his tongue dueling with hers as the kiss deepened. He found himself hardening and he wanted to take her; it killed him that his title forced him to practice restraint. He pulled away reluctantly, resting his forehead against hers; his breathing ragged.

Page 137

"Jade," he murmured. "Let's get married right now, let's not wait."

"And disappoint all the people including my aunt and your sister who want to make a splash?" Jade laughed shakily. "They would never forgive us."

With a heartfelt sigh, he let her go; staring at her while she scooped her hair back on top of her head and secured it with the pins. "I wish you could stay tonight," he said wistfully as she slipped back into her shoes.

"Let's not rock the boat," she came closer to him and laid a hand on his chest feeling the erratic beating of his heart. "They already think I am going to make the worst possible wife for a Pastor so I don't want to give them reason to believe they are right."

John took her hand and kissed it gently." You're going to make the best wife ever," he corrected her. "What are the plans for tomorrow?" he was already running late for a visitation he had to do but he found it hard to tear himself away from her.

"I am going dress shopping with your sister and Aunt Selene and some of the ladies at church want to discuss the menu and what not," she told him with a grimace. "If I call you with an SOS you had better find some sort of an emergency for me to deal with," she warned him.

They left the office together and went their separate ways. He watched as she left the parking lot and watched her car until it was out of sight before he started his engine. He smiled as he turned on his favorite song and started singing along. He had so much to give God thanks for.

*****

When Jade got home, Aunt Selene was sitting on the porch staring out at the garden. It looked like she had been sitting there for a while and Jade wondered if something was wrong. She had told her that she would be home later because she had something to discuss with John.

"Are you okay?" she asked in concern, sitting beside her aunt. It was almost six thirty and the day was still bright out and the pungent scent of the different flowers was heavy on the air.

"I was just out here thinking that you came a short while ago and you'll be leaving." Selene said sadly, her hand absently touching Jade briefly. "I was just sitting here wondering what I am going to do without you here."

"Oh Aunty," Jade exclaimed, hugging the woman. "I am not going anywhere far. I will be here so often that you're going to get tired of seeing me and besides we will see each other at church."

"I know that dear," she smiled briefly. "The house is not going to be same without you in it. I kept wondering recently if I should unbend and accept Benjamin's offer to take him back."

"Do you love him?" Jade asked her.

"I loved him a long time ago but now I am not sure what I feel." Selene gazed off into the garden. "I spent a lot of time pining over him and then one day, I found I was not thinking of him so much."

"Aunty you deserve better than that," Jade said urgently. "You deserve the best and don't do anything because you feel as if you're alone, you're not. I am here and I promise you that I am not going anywhere. I am getting married but I will still be the person you took into your home when I was in so much pain. I will always be grateful to you for finding out that love does not have to hurt and that's what I have discovered with John; so please don't think of it as losing me; think of it as gaining a pastor as a son." She finished with a smile.

Selene patted her hand absently. "Don't mind me dear, I was just wallowing in self pity for a few minutes but I am over it now. The good Lord does not tolerate us feeling sorry for ourselves and as you so aptly put it; I am not losing, I am actually gaining." She gave her niece a gentle squeeze. "So the ladies in the women's fellowship and I were talking and I want you to leave the food planning and decorating to us; we have people who are willing and eager to do that sort of thing."

"Good because John was hinting at forgetting all the planning and get married right now," Jade said teasingly.

"My dear, no!" Selene said in rebuke. "What would people think?"

"Aunty, you know I don't care what people think about me but I finally convinced him that four weeks is not too long to wait." Jade told her.

"Good," Selene said with a sigh of relief. "There has not been a wedding at church since that nice couple Jane and Edmond got married several years ago and this is our Pastor. A lot of people are so excited and darling, I can't tell you how glad I am that he is marrying you. Who would have imagined," she shook her head in wonder.

"God works in mysterious ways," Jade told her with an impish smile.

"He sure does," Selene said seriously. "Come on, let's go get something to eat. I know you told me you would be late but I waited for you so that we may eat together." She stood and waited for her niece to do the same; then linking her arm through hers they made their way to the kitchen. "It's going to be a fabulous wedding you just wait."

*****

Jenna came and picked her up at a quarter to twelve the next day at work. John had gone to visit some people but he had rushed in and kissed her thoroughly, leaving her shivering and aching for more and had left telling her he would see her later.

She had asked a sister to cover for her in the office and left to meet Jenna in the church yard.

"Hurry up," Jenna said impatiently as she stopped to give Brother James a message for someone. "We have a long day ahead of us."

"Kindly remember that I happen to be at work here," Jade told the girl dryly as she climbed in and secured her seatbelt.

"Isn't it different when you're actually sleeping with the boss?" Jenna asked tongue in cheek as she peeled out of the lot.

"Don't even go there," Jade warned, giving the girl a pained look. She was glad to see that she was looking happier these days. She had on jeans and a designer T-shirt and her hair was in its usual ponytail.

"If it wasn't my brother, you would be sharing all the little bedroom secrets with me like how big his, you know what is and how experienced he is in that area," Jenna said with a sigh.

"Jenna!" Jade laughed in spite of herself. She had found herself growing closer and closer and was happy she was going to be her family. "I can tell you this though he is not lacking in that department, I am extremely satisfied."

"Eeyow," Jenna snorted with a grimace. "Way too much information."

"You asked," Jade reminded her.

They got to the shop in less than half an hour and Jenna made a bee line for racks at the back of the store. The owner's name was Lila Parkins; a white woman whose lined face showed signs of aging and she had on too much make-up but was pleasant and accommodating.

"Darling Jenna," she gushed. "How nice to see you!"

"We need to see your best dresses Lila," Jenna said brusquely hurrying ahead with the woman and Jade trailing behind her. Jade saw a side to Jenna that she had had a glimpse of that first morning she had stormed into the office – the rich get what I want side.

"Oh, not for yourself surely?" the woman asked confused.

"No, but you must have heard I am going through a divorce," Jenna said bluntly, stopping by a rack that had a few possibilities.

"Oh dear, I am so sorry," Lila said putting her hands to her ample cheeks.

"Don't be," Jenna waved her comment away. "This is my soon to be sister-in-law," she nodded her head at Jade who was content to keep silent and let Jenna take charge.

"My dear," the woman turned her attention to Jade, her eyes sparkling probably spotting a sure sale. "Pastor John is getting married, praise be to God! I have the perfect dress and you have such a marvelous figure," she hurried away towards the back and an attendant came forward to offer them something to drink. Jenna accepted champagne and she asked for fruit juice ignoring the look Jenna gave her. "I am going back to work after this."

Lila came back with three dresses. One of them Jenna discarded without a second glance saying it was too flouncy and they were not living in the Victorian era. The second one could work but was too hot for a summer wedding. The third one she fell in love with and urged Jade to go try it on. It was perfect. It was close fitting, straight down to the ankles where it flared out gently. It was overlaid with beautiful cream Venetian lace and hugged her curves lovingly. The slightly broad straps that held up the top were pure lace and looked magnificent against her caramel skin. "My dear," Lila breathed, going behind her to hold up her heavy tresses twisting it on top of her head, pulling out two curls against her cheeks. "Absolutely stunning."

"My brother is going to be knocked off his feet," Jenna said staring at the vision of total beauty the girl made. "No veil," she said absently, looking at Jade's face contemplatively. "White rosebuds in her hair and I have just the accessories to go with this. We are going to need shoes."

"Do I have a say in this?" Jade asked mildly as she was told to take off the dress.
"No," Jenna looked surprised that she had actually asked the question. "I told you that this was my area and I would hate to see what you turn up in if it was left up to you."

"I would have you know that I have a very good fashion sense." Jade said highly offended; turning around so that the small pearl like buttons could be undone.

"Of course you do," Jenna said soothingly hurrying off to find the shoes.

They left the store an hour later with the assurance that the dress, shoes and underwear (a white silk almost non-existent teddy) would be delivered to Jenna's house by the end of the week; the dress needed a minor alteration. Jenna had found a green dress and matching shoes suitable for her role as matron of honor and just a shade brighter than her eyes.

Jenna had looked at her hair critically and told her that it needed clipping and she knew just the place when it was nearer to the wedding. Then she went to have lunch. John had called her while they were in the store and told her he was running a little late because he was talking to someone about a funeral.

"Oh Lord, my feet are killing me," Jenna complained as they sat down and placed their order at the pizza place. "But we did get a lot accomplished." She added in satisfaction.

"I never thought I would be doing this again," Jade sipped her water thirstily, the day was uncommonly hot but then again it was getting close to summer so they had to look for anything.

"Is it weird for you?" Jenna asked in concern. She had done what she always did best, thrown herself into other people's affair to try and forget her own and besides, she really liked Jade.

"I love John," she told the girl with a slight smile. "The sad part is I never loved Michael. With John I am able to be myself and not get judged, I can say anything and he won't condemn me and sometimes I am afraid of hurting him; that kind of freedom can really get you on a high that you forget that the person who you can have that freedom with has feelings too."

"I envy you," Jenna said with a sigh, moving her hands so that the waitress could put their pizza before them. "Thanks," she said automatically. "I went into my marriage with eyes wide opened; knowing that I was marrying him for what he had and the power I would have being married to him. For a while I enjoyed what having money and credit cards with no limits can do. But it gets old after a while and especially when the man who gives you that is not at home very much. All that socializing and shopping gets boring after a time."

"Poor little rich girl," Jade commiserated mockingly.

Jenna flicked a piece of cheese at her. "Okay fine, I knew what I was getting myself into; but basically what I am saying is that you and John have the real thing and a lot of people would kill for that including me."

"I do, don't I?" Jade said with a grin, biting into her pizza with enjoyment. "Thanks for everything Jenna, I really appreciate it."

"I am not done yet," she stopped Jade with a look. "I have money and I want to spend it my way. I told you I have a cake person and the wedding will be outdoors at my place so that's that."

"You are one stubborn and determined woman," Jade said shaking her head. "But it's your money who am I to tell you how to spend it."

*****

Jenna dropped her back at the office at a quarter past three and Jade rushed in feeling guilty that she had left Sister Malcolm for so long. But the woman waved away her apologies and told her that it had been her pleasure and she was available anytime to fill in for her. "We all know this is a busy time for you Sister Jade." She said on her way out.

John was in his office on the phone so she did not go in to disturb him. She was typing up the next day's schedule when he came out.

"I want babies," she told him as soon as he came towards her desk. "Maybe two or three. I want to be the mother of your children." He stood stock still and he told himself that maybe he should try and get used to the things that came out of her mouth but she bowled him over every single time.

She came around and stood before him.

"You keep me on my toes," he murmured huskily, pulling her into his arms. "I want babies too and I can't wait to start but first, I want it just to be us. I am not willing to share you with anyone right now, even someone who comes from us." He took her lips with his and Jade melted into his arms.

Chapter 9

"Can you come over?" the voice sounded dull and lifeless and Jade had a hard time placing the voice with the person. It was after ten on a Thursday night and although she was not yet in bed she had put on her pajamas and was idly watching television. Aunt Selene had turned in for the night and she had been sitting in her room trying not to think that her wedding was a week away.

"What's wrong?" Jade demanded. Jenna had been at the office today and she had been perfectly fine.

"I don't want to discuss this over the phone," she told her.

"You want me to leave my house in the middle of the night and come over there. What is it Jenna?" Jade asked impatiently, a little alarmed. She wondered if she should call John but he had been running to and fro all morning and she had urged him to go home and get some sleep, even though he had pleaded with her to spend the night with him.

"It's not the middle of the night and I really need you right now." Jenna said pleadingly.

"Okay fine," Jade sighed. "Give me a few minutes to grab some things and tell Aunt Selene that I will be over at your place."

Jade made short time in reaching the house. Jenna was waiting for her inside the massive front door and she was dressed in very provocative red lingerie.

"You look okay to me," Jade commented, dragging her overnight case from the car and closing the door. "As a matter of fact you look more than okay, you look like a woman who is ready for sex." She swept past her and into the living room where she saw that there were two glasses on the table and an empty bottle of wine. "Being entertaining?" Jade asked with a raised brow.

"It's not what you think," Jenna said hastily.

"What is it then Jenna that had me coming out of my house in the middle of the night?"

"It's not the middle of the night," Jenna protested, taking up the empty glasses and taking them to the kitchen. "I did something really stupid tonight and I am beating myself up over it and I would like my best friend not to judge me."

"If it's not life threatening than I am going to become your ex-best friend," Jade warned, her concern growing. Physically Jenna looked fine so Jade wondered if it had something to do with the wedding.

"I had sex with Barry tonight," she blurted out. They had made their way upstairs to her bedroom and Jade had placed her bag in the corner of the huge room.

"As in your soon to be ex-husband?" Jade asked her; her eyes widening. "No wonder you're dressed like that."

"Please no judgment," Jenna said drearily, climbing on the bed. Jade pull off her jeans and her T-shirt and took the silk pajamas Jenna gave her. "It was all this talk about your wedding and the shopping for the gown and I went and saw about cake. Perfectly delicious by the way."

"You went and chose a cake without me?" Jade asked her in disbelief. "You know what? Never mind continue with the sordid details."

"I called him and asked him to come over. After all, technically he is still my husband and I could not jolly well go and get some random stranger off the streets to satisfy my baser needs now could I?" she asked defensively.

Jade stared at the girl in amazement "Okay, so you had sex with a man that is technically your husband; so what's the problem?"

"We didn't use a condom and because I had been with a man since I threw him out I am in agony as to whether or not I am pregnant." Jenna told her in despair.

"Jenna, I am going to say this only once and I am hoping that you get it." Jade told her slowly. "I am not going to be at your beck and call and you do not get to call me up in the middle of the night and expect me to put aside everything and rush over to be with you." Jade held up a hand as she opened her mouth to say something. "If you say it's not the middle of the night again so help me, I will go downstairs and leave immediately."

"Okay," Jenna said. To Jade's horror she saw that the girl's lips were quivering and her eyes were brimming with tears.

Jade bit her lip wondering if she had been too harsh on her. "Jenna, what's going on?"

The girl burst into tears.

"Honey, what is it?" Jade moved closer and took the distraught girl into her arms.

"I had sex with him Jade and I think I might have feelings for him. What am I going to do?" she cried.

Jade let her cry; not saying anything because right now she did not know what to say. Even after she had finished and her tears were spent Jenna did not move away.

"What are you going to do?" Jade asked her quietly.

Jenna shook her head uncertainly. "He said he has changed and he has given up defending those shady characters and get this: he wants to be baptized in my brother's church and he wants us to have a family. He wants to go into the ministry and do God's work."

Jade eased her up gently and looked at her. "Do you believe him?"

"I don't know," she moved away a little, wiping her cheeks with the back of her hand. Jade had never seen her so vulnerable and lost. She reached for a napkin and handed it to her. "I felt something Jade, something I never felt before. When we made love, it was like being with him for the first time. He wanted to spend the night and I had to force myself to tell him no."

"Are you sure this is not just residual loneliness talking?" Jade asked her.

"What does that even mean?" she asked impatiently. "I felt something for him and I want him back."

"Okay, here's what I think you should do," Jade told her. "Start dating again, get to know each other but take it slow and see if this is something both of you really want. Oh and you can start by inviting him to the wedding."

"The invitations have already been sent out," Jenna fretted, twisting her hands together. "Are you sure you won't mind?"

"What's one more person?" Jade asked softly, seeing the smile bloomed on the girl's face. "Don't rush into anything Jenna; get to know him for real this time."

"We talked for a long time," Jenna mused, staring off into space. "It was not like before and when we made love, I felt as if it was our first time only better and he took his time with me making sure I was satisfied; it was wonderful Jade and for the first time I really felt what the term making love meant."

"Can you forgive him about the affair? I mean totally without bringing it up every two seconds?" Jade asked her.

"What affair?" Jenna asked with a wave of her hand and a slight tilt of her lips. Jade saw the old Jenna returning and she sighed in relief.

"That's good, as long as there can be forgiveness and you can move on from there then I think you're getting there."

"You are going to make one heck of a Pastor's wife," Jenna said in wonder, giving the girl a tight hug. "I am going to take it slow and see where it goes. I have a lot of thinking to do and I guess some praying as well. I have not been doing that a lot these days," she added with a grimace.

"That's the spirit," Jade told her stifling a yawn. "Now, can we get some sleep? I still have work to do at the office you know."

www.SaucyRomanceBooks.com/RomanceBooks

"Okay, although I don't know why you are getting married next week and still working; that's totally ridiculous." Jenna grumbled, scooting over to make room for her.

"Wait a minute," Jade said suddenly. "Was the lovemaking done on this bed?"

Jenna laughed her hand going to her mouth. "No my dear, we did it in the living room and in the kitchen." She said with a grin. "On the floor not on the counter," she said, seeing the look on Jade's face.

*****

The rehearsal dinner was at Aunt Selene's. She and Jenna had had arguments as to where it should be kept.

"My place is way bigger and a lot more convenient," Jenna had argued. She was looking a lot happier and more relaxed and had told Jade that she had been out with Barry two times and it had been wonderful.

Aunt Selene had firmly told her that Jade was like a daughter to her and Jenna was doing so much already she need to let

Page 158

her do this. Jenna had reluctantly acquiesced. Jade had deliberately stayed out of it.

She had spent the night at the cottage. When she had told John that they need to be circumspect and not start any rumors he had almost hit the roof. She had found her replacement and had been coming in three hours a day to show her the ropes but after a few days Sister Bailey was doing fine. She had left John and Jade at the office and she had told him she was leaving come six o'clock because Aunt Selene wanted to discuss the menu with her.

"We haven't spent any time together since the week started Jade, I hate this," he had said impatiently, running agitated fingers through his hair. He had been busy for the past two weeks planning a funeral and making sure that everything was set for the time when he would be absent.

"Calm down," Jade told him mildly. She was sitting on the side of his desk and swinging one leg to and fro. She had dressed casually in jeans and a T-shirt and her hair was in a ponytail, her face devoid of makeup and John thought she looked more like a little girl than the woman he was about to take as his wife. "We have both been busy and you know why."

"You spent the night at my sister's several nights ago and I had to hear it from her," he told her childishly.

"Do you own me now?" she asked him with an arched brow. She had not told him about Jenna wanting to get back with her husband although she had wanted to but it was not hers to tell. She was not going to hold back anything from him but that had to come from Jenna herself.

"I can't believe you just said that," he stared at her, a hurt expression on his face.

With a sigh, Jade slid off the desk and came around to sit on his lap. "I am sorry," she told him, smoothing the frown from his brow. "This up and down and almost planning a wedding is getting to me."

"Almost?" he raised a brow, a slight smile tugging at his lips. "Your sister has taken over completely," Jade told him with a sheepish grin. "I really don't mind much but at some point I would like to have an input. That girl is like a child in a candy store."

He laughed. "Jenna loves planning things, even when she was little she always offered to plan birthday parties and things like that." He looked at her with love glowing in his startling green eyes. "I am glad you two are friends."

"So am I," Jade said sincerely. "I never really had friends before so this thing I have with Jenna, even though she makes me want to box her ears sometimes, is something that I love."

"I love you Jade," he said suddenly.

"I know," Jade told him softly, resting her head against his forehead. She lifted his strong chin and gazed at him. "I can't wait to marry you," she murmured bringing her lips down to meet his. With a groan he opened his mouth and took hers; his tongue meeting hers. Jade dug her fingers in his hair and bore him back against the seat, deepening the kiss.

John gripped her waist and pulled her closer, his hands holding her steady as he devoured her mouth. "Come home with me tonight," he dragged his mouth from hers; his breathing ragged.

She shook her head, reaching for his mouth again; hungry for him; but he evaded her. "Why not?" he asked frustration rife in his tone.

"Because we have to behave circumspect and I have to remember that you are the Pastor."

"Jade I need you," he told her tightly. "Feel this," he took her hand and placed it on his crotch. His erection was rubbing tightly inside his jeans and Jade could not move her hand away. "I get an erection just looking at you," he continued grimly. "I have to be praying constantly for God to give me the restraint I need when I am doing something else. I need you now and I need to spend the night with you tonight."

Jade felt the thrill run through her body at his words. He made her feel as if she was the only woman in the world and the feeling was heady.

"I'll come home with you," she told him, her hand rubbing against him.

"It has to be now," he said hoarsely. "It has to be now," he repeated as she pulled down his zipper and reached inside to touch him and caress his manhood. His mouth crushed hers with a stunning force that left her breathless and for several minutes they did not say anything else.

She had left very early the next morning to go home and Aunt Selene had made a list of some things she thought could do for the food items.

"I was thinking we would do the cooking at the house since Jenna has that lovely kitchen that has not been used," Selene said dryly. She was hurrying to leave for work as she planned on coming home early to get started for the rehearsal dinner. "And since the wedding will be outdoors and the weather seems like it's going to be lovely, we are thinking of serving lots of cool drinks and cut down on the heavy food so to speak. So the ladies at church and of course Jenna," she rolled her eyes expressively. "We decided to go with lots of salad and fruit bowls and of course some shrimp cocktail and maybe a little roast pork and some barbecue chicken. How does that sound dear?"

"Aunty you know when it comes to preparing food that's your area and I have no intention of interfering or having any input; I am just so grateful for all the help." Jade hugged her fondly.

"You're welcome dear," Aunt Selene returned the hug. "I'm running a little late so I'll see you later. I take it you'll be going to the hairdresser with Jenna?"

"Oh my goodness!" Jade exclaimed. "I had totally forgotten about that and no doubt she will be swinging by shortly to pick me up. Thanks Aunty." She called as she hurried upstairs to shower and get ready.

Jenna came by for her at a quarter to eleven and they went to the hairdresser that did her hair. He was male and so obviously gay that Jade found herself laughing as he exclaimed over her abundant tresses and how some women would kill to have hair like hers. He refused to cut off a lot saying it was a sin to put scissors in hair as beautiful as hers. He just shaped up the front and sides and a little from the back and asked what was the arrangement for the wedding.

"She will be wearing tiny rosebuds on the sides Marco," Jenna told him.

"Oh darling, wonderful idea!" he gushed. "No need to hide this gorgeous tresses with a tiresome veil; so last season," he ended with a grimace. "I'll just do a sweep on top of the crown and let the gel do the magic." He plucked her brows and rubbed some special cream on her face and neck. "To open up the pores," he told her.

Next he dealt with Jenna, clipping off some of her blonde tresses and regaling her with the latest gossip. "Girl, I see you have gotten back with that husband of yours," he commented.

"Who told you that?" Jenna asked him sharply, her eyes meeting his in the large mirror.

"Marco has ears everywhere darling," he told her with an impish grin; his large dark eyes twinkling. He was totally bald and muscles rippled in his arms as he handled the scissors deftly. He was wearing impossibly tight pink jeans and an outrageously orange shirt.

"What do you think?" she asked him a little anxiously.

"Girl, take back your man and don't care what anybody wants to say," he had started brushing her hair vigorously. "You are the one who is going to live with him but make sure and tell him that if he points his penis at another woman again you are going to hack it off."

There was laughter in the salon after the first moment of shocked silence and Jenna and Jade left there shortly after. He had given them small gift bags of make-up and had instructed them how to apply it.

*****

The rehearsal dinner was wonderful and the food outstanding. Aunt Selene had opted to do it outdoors and she had placed lights on the porch and in the shrubbery and it looked fantastic. There were not a lot of people invited so she had used one long table. Deacon Brown and his wife Marion had come along with Brother Sean who was going to be best man and there was Sister Bailey and Sister Baker who were in charge of the catering and of course Jenna and John and Jade had told Jenna to invite Barry as well. She had met him the day before when Jenna had taken her to go and look at the cake and she had to admit she liked him. He was tall and dark with dark hair and piercing gray eyes that seemed to see right through you and he had a gentle knowing smile and had eyes only for Jenna. Jade had been a little apprehensive as to whether or not John would welcome him back but John, although a little detached, had been okay with him being there.

Jade had dressed in a simple pink dress that swayed seductively against her body and left her arms and shoulders bare. "Do you seriously expect me to behave tonight?" John had whispered in her ear as he pulled her in his arms from behind.

The food was mostly finger food and there was champagne and toasts. A particularly tearful one from Aunt Selene, who said that the place was not going to be the same without Jade, but she was so happy that she was going to have Pastor John not only as her pastor but as her son as well.

The party broke up at nine thirty and Jade went upstairs to change and grab her overnight case. She had moved most of her things from her room over to John's at the beginning of the week and had only a few items left.

"Having second thoughts?" his deep voice sounded from the doorway.

"Not a chance," Jade told him immediately. "Aren't you supposed to be on your way home?" she asked him coming over and putting her arms around his neck.

"I couldn't leave without telling you a proper goodbye." He murmured, tipping her chin up to look into her eyes.

"Is that so?"

"Hmm," he took her lips in a gentle kiss. "I can't wait for tomorrow." He whispered as he kissed her hungrily. "Then you'll be my wife."

Chapter 10

The day of the wedding dawned bright and sunny. It promised to be a glorious day even though it had sprinkled the night before. By mid morning, the water that had been glistening on the plants had all but dried up.

Jenna had woken her up at nine o'clock but Jade had been awake from seven and had even spoken to John earlier. He had called to tell her that he loved her and couldn't wait until she was Mrs. John Wynter. Her heart had raced at that and she had smiled and told him she could not wait either. The wedding was set for one o'clock sharp and since everything was being done at the house there was no need to hurry. They were having breakfast together. When Jade went downstairs, Jenna was in the kitchen, some sort of cream on her face and she had on a ratty T-shirt and there were two bowls of cereals, glasses of orange juice and croissants and cups of black coffee. "Wow you did all this?" she asked teasingly as she pulled out a chair.

"That's about the extent of my culinary skills," she said as she joined Jade. "So eat up and you're supposed to take a long leisurely bubble bath; I put some bath salts in as you'll be using my bathroom and then I will do your hair as well as your make-up." She looked at Jade critically as she sipped her coffee. "Your skin is so flawless; if you weren't getting married to my brother I would hate you."

"Thanks, I think" Jade told her with a grin. "So where is Barry? I thought he was spending the night."

"No, taking it slow remember?" Jenna bit into her bagel with appreciation. "He is agreeing and we are taking baby steps. He spoke to John and my brother is kind of guarded. I guess he's taking it slow too."

They finished breakfast and Jenna ordered her to go upstairs and take her bath. Jade went without protest. The bathroom was two times the size of her room at Aunt Selene's and had mirrors all around. It had black and white marble floors and the claw footed bath was white and large enough to hold half a dozen people.

Jade stepped into the warm scented water and slid down in appreciation as the suds closed over her; resting her head against the towel that had been placed there and closed her eyes, relaxing as the combination of the warmth and the intoxicating scent coming from the water lulled her into complacency.

She did not realize that she had dozed off a little until she heard Jenna calling her name. She opened her eyes to see the girl standing beside the bath and looking at her in amusement. "Too relaxing for you?"

"Much," Jade said ruefully as she reached for the towel Jenna handed her. "What time is it?"

"Some minutes to eleven," Jenna said airily.

"I have been in here for more than an hour!" Jade was astounded.

"Relax," Jenna said with a wave of her hand as she went towards the bedroom. "You have all the time in the world and by the way my pesky brother and your soon to be husband called two times while you were in the bath and wanted to talk to you. He nearly bit my head off when I told him you weren't available."

"Jenna, why didn't you come and let me talk to him?" Jade followed her into the bedroom, her forehead creased into a frown.

"Seriously?" she rounded on her. "You two are behaving as if you're teenagers instead of grown people. You will be seeing each other in what," she glanced at the jeweled clock on the wall. "Oh look at that! In precisely two hours. What could you possibly have to talk about now and I know he called you this morning already. The sooner you two get married, the better." She flounced away and Jade grinned as she took off the towel and slipped into the silk teddy she had gotten from the bridal store. She would have called John back but she had left her phone in the kitchen. She was creaming her skin with the highly expensive scented cream when Jenna came back in. She had already showered and her hair already done because she wanted to concentrate on Jade.

"I have always wanted a sister," Jade commented as soon as she sat in front of the huge dressing table with Jenna behind her ready to do her hair. Their eyes met in the mirror and Jade saw the telltale emotion on her face.

"Don't you dare make me ruin my make-up after I spent half an hour applying it," she threatened. "You have got one now." She added softly hugging Jade from behind. "Now let's go get you married to my brother." She said briskly.

Jenna was very efficient with the comb and brush and in short order she had brushed Jade's curls and twisted it into a smooth chignon on top of her head, securing it with pins. She then placed the small rosebuds with green leaves at both sides of her hair. The upswept style threw Jade's face into sharp relief; revealing all the delicate angles and planes and her beautiful bone structure. She did not require much makeup so Jenna went for the bare minimal. Her beauty was greatly highlighted and the rose color lip gloss shimmered causing her lips to be more pronounced. "My Lord you are stunning," Jenna breathed, stepping back to look at the girl.

They heard a slight noise downstairs and Jenna went to the top of the stairs to find out what it was. There had been people milling around all morning getting the gazebo ready and making sure the chairs were placed properly and there also the ladies in the kitchen preparing the meal.

It was Aunt Selene and she was already dressed in a soft shell pink skirt suit and matching shoes. "I wanted to see you get dressed, I could not stay away." She came into the bedroom, her eyes riveted on the lovely girl. "You look like you just stepped out of a bridal magazine," she murmured, her eyes misting over. "I wish my sister could have seen you."

"So do I Aunty," Jade said a little sadly, giving the woman a hug. She helped Jenna with Jade's dress and did the several tiny buttons at the back. "My dear you are stunning!"

"I agree," Jenna said with a smile, moving forward to adjust one of the curls falling on her cheek. "There now it's perfect."

They went downstairs together and sat waiting in the large living room while people filled up the chairs. Deacon Brown was already standing at his place at the gazebo and a few minutes to one the groom came and took his place. Then it was time for the orchestra to start the cue and Jenna went out on the arms of the best man. There was a hush of expectancy as the people stood and the music changed to the wedding march. Jenna's husband had offered to walk her up the aisle and they moved slowly upwards. Jade was conscious of the many eyes on her but she did not have eyes for anyone except John who stood there; in his pearl gray suit and his hair glinting in the sunlight. He came halfway to meet her, his eyes touching on Barry briefly as he took her arm in his; his other hand closing over hers possessively.

He did not speak but his eyes spoke volumes and Jade felt a catch inside her throat.

Deacon Brown beckoned for the crowd to sit. "Friends and family we are gathered here this beautiful afternoon to witness the love of two people: our dear pastor John and our sister Jade. Love is a beautiful equalizer and has finally caught up with our pastor," he waited until the laughter had stopped. "I have to ask the question that if there is anyone here who thinks that this man and this woman should not be wed let them speak now or forever hold their peace." He waited a spell and then he continued. "The couple would like to say their own vows." He stepped back and John turned to Jade holding both her hands.

"Jade, it's simple. I have found the one that I want to spend the rest of my life with. I have found the person I want to grow old with, have children with and laugh and cry with. I have found the one that I want to spend my good days and my bad days with and that person is you. It has to be you and no matter what happens it will always be you. I love you beyond measure and it's God first and then you."

"John," Jade had to clear her throat to continue. "I never knew it could ever be like this. I wake up each morning wondering if I am dreaming; is this real? I love you so much that I cannot ever find the words to tell you how much and I will spend the rest of my days telling you and showing you how much. I will respect you and honor you as my husband for as long as we both shall live." His hands tightened on hers and he had to use supreme effort not to crush her into his arms.

"Now it's my turn," Deacon Brown stepped forward. "John Anthony Wynter do you take Jade Elizabeth Reid to be your lawful wedded wife till death do you part?"

"I do," John's voice was clear and resounding.

"Jade Elizabeth Reid do you take John Anthony Wynter to be your lawfully wedded husband to have and to hold until death do you part?"

"I do," Jade said looking up at him.

"The rings please." Deacon Brown said to the best man; waiting while they exchanged rings.

"Let us pray our blessings on this couple." Deacon Brown instructed. "Heavenly Father, the creator of life and of marriage, we place your daughter and son into your hands to guide them and lead them in the right direction. We ask for your blessings on them and ask that as they take this very honorable step towards the future that you will be with them every step of the way. Amen."

"Now by the powers vested in me, I now pronounce you husband and wife. You may kiss your bride Pastor John," Before the words were even out of Deacon Brown's mouth properly Jade was already in John's arms as he kissed her with all the pent up emotions he was feeling.

"Ladies and Gentlemen, I give you Mr. and Mrs. John Wynter." John released her; his hands shaking as he turned to face everyone. He pulled her close to his side as they made their way down the aisle.

They were stopped on the way several times by people wishing them all the best and the members of the church welcoming her to the fold. Beside her, she could feel John's impatience and she had to hide a smile as she greeted yet another well wisher. They finally made it to the head table which was just a few feet away in Jenna's colorful garden. The cake rose magnificently on a side table and the main table was decorated with balloons and green and white crepe paper.

They seated themselves, with John holding out the chair for her and prayer was said before the meal begun. Jade watched with appreciation as both Jenna and Aunt Selene subtly indicated what and when to serve. Champagnes were poured seemingly unceasingly and toasts were made. Then it was time for the groom's toast and John stood up. "My family and friends; on behalf of my wife and I," he paused as there was a thunderous applause and hooting. "I would like to thank you for making this evening a very successful one. My wife and I," he grinned as he said it again, "had very little to with the arrangements. We were told to just show up and I want to especially thank my sister Jenna who took over," he glanced over at his sister who stuck her tongue out. "And dear Aunt Selene and members of the church who went above and beyond to make this evening what it is. In so saying, I have to admit that as beautiful as the ceremony is I am going to urge you to eat fast and get it over and done with so that my wife and I can get on with the business of being married." There was laughter all around as he sat.

Jade gave him a wry look, "My wife and I?" she asked him teasingly.

"I am going to be saying it every chance I get," he told her mildly, leaning over to kiss her lingeringly on the lips.

They had the cutting of the cake and their first dance as husband and wife and then it was time to go inside. They had been generously given the place for a week to relax and use all the amenities and consider it a honeymoon/vacation. Jenna had even stocked the place with all sorts of meals that were easy to prepare. "In case you guys don't feel like getting out of bed," she had said with a wink.

"Darling, I am so proud of you," Aunt Selene came over and hugged her tightly. "And Pastor John welcome to the family." She hugged him.

"Thanks Aunt Selene," he said softly. "But I wish you would call me John."
"It will take some getting used to," she told him with a smile.

Jenna came over after hugging first Jade and then her brother. Jade saw how Barry could not take his eyes off her. She wore the green silk dress well and her blonde hair was caught at the nape of her neck and emeralds glinted at her earlobes. "My sister," she murmured, and then she turned to her brother. "Take care of her or you answer to me." She warned, and then with a grin she kissed his cheek.

Finally everyone had left, even the ones who had been doing the cleaning up. The large heap of wedding gifts was stacked in the living room and the cake and left over food were in the kitchen.

He lifted her and carried her up the winding staircase and did not set her down until they were in the huge bedroom. Jade's eyes widened in surprise. They were rose petals strewn over the delicate pink comforter on the massive king sized bed and a bucket with a bottle of champagne chilling on the side table along with two glasses and a bowl of fruit and a plate with shrimp cocktail. There was also a note: "To be enjoyed in between sex. Love Jenna".

"Your sister is amazing," Jade told him as he came behind her and read the note. "And totally intrusive," he added dryly.

"Do you want to eat something?" she asked him turning to face him.

"Yes," he murmured, his meaning clear as he stared at her mouth hungrily.

"You're terrible," she rebuked softly, twining her arms around his neck.

"My wife," he whispered, ducking his head to take her mouth with his. Jade had taken off her shoes and she had to go on her toes to reach him. She opened her mouth to give him better access and he groaned as he deepened the kiss; his hands tightening its hold on her. With a sudden movement and without removing his mouth from hers he lifted her and put her on the bed. She pulled away from him.

"I want to feel your body," she said urgently. He turned her around to undo the many small pearl buttons on the back of the dress. Halfway down she heard him groaning with impatience. "This is torture," he said tightly. But finally, he had finished undoing them and he eased off her dress, his eyes widening as he saw the delicate and revealing undergarment. He gently put the dress aside and hurriedly took off his clothes leaving his underwear.

"You're so beautiful," he whispered, his hands running the length of her body.

"John please," she was moving restlessly as his hand lingered on her pubic area that was imprinted through the sheer white material.

"I know baby," he bent his head and took her mouth with his, starting out slow as he kissed her thoroughly, his tongue moving against hers. Jade pushed her fingers through his hair and held on to him; her body moving against his urgently, feeling his erection against her. He broke off the kiss and went downwards to her breasts where he peeled off the material; exposing her; the nipples as hard as pebbles. He took one into his mouth; teasing it; his tongue licking causing her to squirm and then he went on to the next one before making his way down towards her flat stomach; his tongue reaching inside her navel before going further down where he kissed on top of her pubic area. Jade's hips arched as his tongue delved inside her. He held onto her hips and lifted her as he titillate her with his tongue ruthlessly until she was begging him to take her. He heeded her cries and came over her, suspended for a while as he looked at her face flushed with passion and need.

"Tell me you love me," he muttered. He had taken off his underwear and his penis pulsed with the need of her.

"I love you, please John" she said huskily.

Without another word he entered her, easing inside her slowly, not wanting to hurt her and yet impatient to feel her around him. Jade enveloped him like a glove and he groaned harshly as he went deeper, wanting to feel all of her. Then he started moving and as she moved with him he increased the tempo; their bodies moving together in unison. He changed position abruptly as she wrapped her legs around his waist and he pulled her up against him; allowing her to sit on him; his eyes darkening as her eyes widened. He stopped and looked at her; his expression stormy. "I love you so much that I don't know where you left off and I begin," he told her hoarsely. He held her hips firmly and rotate his hips causing her to gasp as he filled her up and then his thrust deepened and Jade held onto him tightly as his control slipped and he pulled her legs up and over; his thrusts frantic and hurried as if he could not get enough of her. Jade raised her legs and put them up against his shoulders; she was almost delirious with the pleasure that was erupting from her body. They came together and it was like an explosion inside their bodies. Jade heard him cry out her name over and over again; his voice anguished. She held him to her, her body shaking uncontrollably as she waited for the maelstrom to finish.

They were silent for a long time; trying to digest what had just happened. Then Jade spoke. She was still gathered close into his arms and his body was still shaking. His penis was still semi erect inside her and she did not want him to move. "I have never felt like this before," she murmured, running a finger up and down his chest hair that was slightly damp. "I get scared at the extent of how much I love you and I keep wondering what I would do if something happens to you."

He brushed back her hair which had become undone and was tangled against her cheeks. "I spent all my life in the ministry and I was satisfied and contented with doing that and a lot of people thought it strange that I did not find a nice girl and settled down." He smiled slightly, his hands tightening around her waist. "But I always told myself that I was not willing to just settle and that's what a lot of people do Jade, they settle because maybe time is running out but I was waiting for you; for this and I am glad I did."

"I am glad you waited," she whispered softly. "God has given me a chance to love and for that I will be eternally grateful to him. This makes up for the pain and humiliation I suffered before and if I had known that this was my light at the end of the tunnel, I would have borne it without complaint. I love you so much my husband."

"I love you too baby; very much." He whispered achingly and he spent the greater part of the night showing her how much.

The end.

If you enjoyed this ebook and want me to keep writing more, please leave a review of it on the store where you bought it. By doing so you'll allow me more time to write these books for you as they'll get more exposure. So thank you. :)

Get Free Romance eBooks!

Hi there. As a special thank you for buying this book, for a limited time I want to send you some great ebooks completely **free of charge** directly to your email! You can get it by going to this page:

www.SaucyRomanceBooks.com/RomanceBooks

www.saucyromancebooks.com/physical

You can see a the cover of these books on the next page:

ONE LONE COWBOY, ONE WOMAN ON A MISSION...

THE LONE ★ COWBOY

EMILY J

ROCHELLE

IF IT'S MEANT TO BE...

Him

KIMBERLY GREENFORD

IRE MET HIS MATCH?

UCH LASS

LDING

PLAYER GONNA PLAY?

SHE'S THE ONE HE WANTS BUT CAN SHE TRUST HIM?

ONE VAMPIRE. ONE COP. ONE LOVE.

VAMPIRES OF CLEARVIEW

J A FIELDING

These ebooks are so exclusive you can't even buy them.
When you download them I'll also send you updates when
new books like this are available.

Again, that link is:

www.saucyromancebooks.com/physical

Now, if you enjoyed the book you just read, please leave a
positive review of it where you bought it (e.g. Amazon). It'll
help get it out there a lot more and mean I can continue writing
these books for you. So thank you. :)

More Books By Shannon Gardener

If you like this story, you'll love Shannon Gardener's other
BWWM Christian romance stories (search ' Shannon
Gardener bwwm' on Amazon to see them).

Here's a preview of one of them, 'The Singer':

Mary had not wanted to go – but her friends had dragged her out of her one bedroom apartment and insisted that she needed to get on with her life. It had been six months since her and Darrell had broken their engagement and he had moved on so she need to as well. She had gotten dressed just to shut them up – all the while grumbling that she had no idea what going to a church concert would accomplish. So she had gone and Claudette and April had told her that she kind of looked like her old self again.

The church was small and quaint and had a warm family feeling to it. There had been no available seats at the back so they had been forced to sit at the front and endure all the eyes staring at them.

The choir had been singing with a hot lead singer – the song: "Amazing Grace" and Mary had been transformed as he did the solo piece – the man can sing. Not bad for a white man! She thought.

They had fun. There was a skit depicting David and Goliath which turned out to be very funny and some poems and the choir performed several times. She wanted to hear him sing all the time. His voice was amazing.

There was a meet and greet outside the chapel and he was a part of it. He had taken off his choir robe and was in jeans and a T-shirt.

"I love your singing," she told him as he took her hand in his.

"Thanks; to God be the glory," he told her, holding onto her hand for a little while longer. "This your first time at Heaven's chapel?"

"Yes," she pulled her hand away from him a little self-consciously; fully aware that they were holding up the procession and she could see that her friends were looking at her curiously. "I attend The Baptist Church in town.

"So can we look forward to seeing you again?" he asked her, not in any hurry to stop talking to her. He was very handsome with dark brown hair and hazel eyes with ridiculously long lashes.

"I don't know, I guess so." Mary felt flustered and she wanted to leave immediately.

"I look forward to seeing you again." He told her softly as he turned his charming smile on another visitor.

"What was that all about?" April asked as they made their way towards her car. Her friend had been the one to introduce her to Darrell and was determined to protect her from future heartbreak.

"What?" Mary opened the passenger side of the car and got in hastily, sneaking one last look at the cute chorister. He was still greeting people but for one moment their eyes met and held and he smiled and waved at her. Mary averted her eyes quickly, praying that her friends had not noticed.

"You know what," April pulled away from the curb; sparing her friend a quizzical glance – "Did you notice how he held on to Mary's hand longer than the others, Claudette?" she sought confirmation from their friend in the back seat.

"Of course I did, I also saw him reach under her blouse to fondle her breast." Claudette said dryly with an impatient shake of her curly hair. "You read something into every little thing April. The man was just being friendly."

"I know what I saw." April sniffed in offense. "He was definitely checking her out."

The other two girls refused to accommodate her and the short journey continued in silence much to Mary's relief.

They dropped her off at her apartment and went on their way with a promise to meet up for lunch sometime next week.

Mary's apartment was more serviceable rather than luxurious. It was quite small – one bedroom with a small balcony that she had used to plant tomatoes and green peas and some crocuses. There was a small table and two chairs where she had most of her solitary meals. Eight months ago she had expected to be married and moved to a three bedroom town house but that dream had evaporated into thin air when Darrell had told her that they were not compatible – he being a lawyer and she being a kindergarten teacher; they really had nothing in common. He had gone off to a big law firm and was now dating one of the partner's daughters. So much for love; she thought wearily. But now that she stopped to think about it – had they really love each other? Or were they pushed together by their parents? Her parents had had dreams of her being married to a doctor or a lawyer and when Darrell had started attending First Town Baptist they had been in corporate heaven! He was a black man going places and she needed to go there with him, they had told her – they were right. He was really going places, without her! Suffice it to say, they had blamed her for the break up and told her how she had let a fine man like Darrell get away from her.

Kicking off her shoes she went into the tiny kitchen to make herself a cup of chamomile tea. Tomorrow was Sunday and she had Sunday school to teach and she needed her sleep.

*****

Charles gave the table a final polish and stepped back to admire the sheen. He had acquired the antique cherry table at an auction and had decided that it was just what he needed. He was planning to put recent bestsellers on the table so that peoples eyes would gravitate towards it as they opened the door. His concentration was interrupted by the chiming of the doorbell. With a quick smile he put away his dust cloth and went out to meet his latest customer. His smile brightened as he realized that it was the girl who had been at the service last Sunday evening.

"Hi there! Nice to see you again." He told her.

Mary gave a startled glance over at the sound of the voice, she had been doing a little browsing and admiring the quaint little shop and wondering to herself why she had never been inside before. It was him! She realized with a little quickening of her pulse – the singer from that church.

"Hello, fancy seeing you here." She took his outstretched hand with a smile.

"I was kind of hoping we would run into each other again," he said sheepishly; his charming smile crinkling his hazel eyes and those lashes!

Mary wished she had on something sexier than black pants and white dress shirt – which now after spending several hours with fourteen preschoolers looked bedraggled and a little wrinkled and she smelled of play dough and crayons. At least her shoulder length black curls were in a tidy bun on top of her head.

"Don't tell me, you want to recruit me to be a part of the choir."
She grinned at him; and as before, she was the one who had
to pull away her hand.

"That's part of it." He told her impishly, taking her arm and
leading her to a small alcove by the window. "Coffee?"

"Now I know why this place is called 'Books and Coffee'.
Couldn't come up with a better name?" she smiled, arching
one delicate brow.

"I would have you know that this place have been around for
generations of Duncan's and the name suits." He placed a
steaming cup of coffee on the table in front of her along with
cream and sugar. "That is how we have become the number
one bookstore in this area. We treat our customers to more
than books – a little hot beverage, internet browsing and
excellent conversation." He sat right across from her, his
hands dangerously near to hers on the small table.

"You being the conversant, I take it?" she stirred the small
amount of sugar into her coffee, more to give her hands
something to do – he was making her jittery.

"What do you think?" he smiled that infectious smile at her that caused her to smile in return. Suddenly he leaned forward and brushed something off her cheek. Mary froze as the very simple touch of his finger felt as if he had touched her with his lips. Get a grip girl! She chided herself.

"Paint smear." He told her casually. If he noticed her unusual reaction he showed no sign of it – reaching for a napkin to wipe his fingers.

"One of the hazards of being a kindergarten teacher," Mary forced herself to be nonchalant. She must be some kind of a ninny to let a simple touch of a stranger's fingers practically turn her into a mass of Jell-O! "My name is Mary Bennett, by the way and I actually came in to look for a New Revised Standard Version Bible."

"Charles Duncan, at your service." He gave a small bow as he stood up; moving away from the table; going to one of the bookshelves. "Charles Duncan, very nice to meet you." He flashed her another heartbreaking smile. "So you are a teacher. How do you like it?"

"I love it." Mary told him, her eyes lighting up in appreciation as she sipped her coffee. "This is very good coffee. Now I know what you do, if they don't come back to buy books they come for the coffee."

"Now you catch on." Charles told her as he came over with the Bible she had ordered. "This the one?" At her nod, he went over to the cash register and rang up the sale.

"So Mary, any significant other?" the casualness of his voice belied the importance of the question. But Mary did not hesitate to respond; she had a feeling that her answer was crucial.

"No." she said softly – her hands wrapping around the coffee cup as if seeking the warmth of it.

"Good," he told her briskly, bagging up her purchase in a quaint little white bag that had the words emblazoned on it: "Books & Coffee" – We serve you in so many ways."

"Cute," Mary took her bag and handed him her credit card.

"I came up with the slogan" he grinned impishly as he took the card from her. For a little while she sat savoring the excellent coffee and the very handsome man with the ready smile. Another customer had come in and he was serving her – an elderly woman with white hair who seemed to be a regular customer. Every now and then he would look over to her and flash that smile, making her feel as if she was the most important person around. It was heady! She wanted to stay for a lot longer but did not want it to be too obvious – she felt relaxed and comfortable but she had lessons to plan and she really needed to go home; today being Thursday, she had activities to plan for tomorrow. Picking up her package, she stood up getting ready to leave. He immediately excused himself from the elderly lady and came over to her. "Leaving?" he asked her; his expression registering disappointment.

"I have to," she took the hand he put forward and felt the same jolt of awareness as before but this time she let his touch lingered. "Lessons to prepare."

"I hope you will come again and keep coming." He told her with a gentle squeeze. "My business card is in the bag. – call if you suddenly decide that you need something to read or another Bible. Just write your number on this card, you know in case I come upon something that might interest you for the kids you teach." He smiled as he handed her the paper to write her number. "And Mary," he pulled away his hand reluctantly. "There is no other significant other for me." He opened the door for her; his smile flashing automatically. She lingered a little before leaving with a reluctance that left her feeling confused. He was certainly getting under her skin!

She went home but preparing her lesson plan and creating some sort of activities was very far from her mind. She kept reliving the evening over and over again – his smile, the play of his feminine lashes playing on his cheekbones when he looked down and his touch! She found herself shivering just remembering his lingering touch on her hands and most of all how he had told her that he was available! He had not said it in so many words but she knew what he meant. She remembered his dark brown hair, curling slightly on the top and the way his shirt hugged his slight yet muscular frame – shrugging aside her thoughts which were suddenly becoming too provocative she deliberately turned her attention to the job at hand – she had rabbits to make and a collage of all her students to create. Thinking about Charles Duncan was not something she should be doing...

*

If you want to read the rest, search 'The Singer Shannon Gardener' on Amazon.

You can also see other related books by myself and other top romance authors at:

www.saucyromancebooks.com/romancebooks

CPSIA information can be obtained
at www.ICGtesting.com
Printed in the USA
LVHW05s2333080618
580208LV00008B/167/P